Louis A. Banks

Heroic Personalities

Louis A. Banks

Heroic Personalities

ISBN/EAN: 9783337196141

Printed in Europe, USA, Canada, Australia, Japan

Cover: Foto ©Andreas Hilbeck / pixelio.de

More available books at **www.hansebooks.com**

HEROIC PERSONALITIES

BY

LOUIS ALBERT BANKS, D.D.

Author of "The Christ Brotherhood," "Immortal Hymns
and Their Story," "Christ and His Friends," Etc.

NEW YORK: EATON & MAINS
CINCINNATI: CURTS & JENNINGS

by
EATON & MAINS,
1898.

EATON & MAINS PRESS,
150 Fifth Avenue, New York.

To
My Friend and Hero,
The Hon. William W. Smith,
This Volume is
Affectionately Dedicated
By the Author.

CONTENTS.

LIST OF ILLUSTRATIONS.

HEROIC
PERSONALITIES.

I.

A Heroic Business Career.

SOME forty years ago a young man began his life work as a confectioner in the city of Poughkeepsie, N. Y. His mother was a widow, and he had a very small capital, but he was a brave-hearted youth, and set himself to work with courage and good will. He would make his candy himself, and then, with his basket on his arm, travel the round of the stores and any private houses where his goods had been ordered. He determined from the first that his candy should always be the very best he could make. He was scrupulously clean. Although his clothes were plain, his linen and his long white aprons were white as snow. One day a gentleman complimented him on the fact of his always being so neat

and clean about his person and business.
The boy flushed with pleasure under the
compliment, but answered, with a pride that
spoke volumes for his filial devotion, "That,
sir, is the work of my mother."

Hon. Wm. W. Smith.

The outward cleanliness of this youth was
only a suggestion of the inward purity and
wholesomeness of his strong young soul.
He early became a sincere Christian, and
made a solemn determination that, no mat-

ter what was the result, he would live up to his Christianity in all the business engagements of his life, and registered a vow that if the time ever came when he either had to lose business or sacrifice his Christian principle, it should be his business and not his Christianity that should suffer.

A testing time came soon enough. One of his friends, who was also one of the richest young men in the community and the best customer he had, came to his shop one day and ordered ten pounds of brandy drops. The young confectioner did not make these, but he ordered them from New York by express. Before they came, however, his conscience began to trouble him. Was he doing right in having a hand in selling these brandy candies? He knew that the young man who had ordered them would give them out among the young men and the young women of his acquaintance, and it might be that more than one would get their first taste of intoxicating drink in that way, and no one could tell what sad result would come of it. On the other hand, if he refused to accommodate his customer, he would no doubt lose his friendship and his trade, and only drive him to some one else who would procure the desired confections for him. He could not sleep that night, and the more he thought about it the more thoroughly convinced he became that it was not a Christian thing to in any way have part in putting temptation in the path of another. Having come to this conclusion, he acted with promptness and firmness. When the brandy drops came he immediately expressed them back to the wholesale firm in New York, and when the young man came after them he frankly told him what he had done, and why. As he expected, the young man was very angry, and was full of contempt for him on account of what he called his "fanatical notions."

That was the parting of the ways for these two young men. The poor young confectioner that stood by his principles has grown to be a wealthy and honored citizen, while the rich young tippler has long since gone to a dishonored grave, eaten up by his sinful lusts and appetites, as Herod was eaten of worms.

Our young hero maintained the same attitude as his business enlarged and broadened. He became after a while a caterer, and on his business cards, through all the years, he has kept the plain and simple statement that not only will no wines and liquors be furnished by him, but he will not permit his employees to serve at a feast or dinner where they are used. He has many times lost thousands of dollars by this fidelity to principle, but it has never tempted him to swerve for a moment, and, perhaps, in the long run, he has gained by it even financially. His splendid fidelity to principle has been a great object lesson to all who have known him, and has helped by example and influence to banish the punch bowl and the wineglass from many a wedding feast and public dinner in that part of the country.

When the great Poughkeepsie railroad bridge was nearing completion a dinner was given to the railroad men of the country at that place. Our friend, as the leading

caterer of the region, was secured for the occasion. But as the time drew near and he
found they intended to use wines he refused
absolutely to have anything to do with it,
and so steadfastly did he abide by his purpose that the wines were banished.

A magnificent public park in Poughkeepsie, an Old Ladies' Home building, and many
other monuments of his philanthropy bear
witness that his generosity is as conspicuous
a trait as his heroic devotion to principle.

Who can tell how wide is the influence for
good which such a business man spreads
through the community? Like Peter's heal-
ing shadow, on whomsoever the influence of
such a man falls, its effect is to strengthen
him in purity and righteousness of life. All
honor to Hon. William W. Smith, the heroic
business man of Poughkeepsie!

II.

The Shepherdess of the Black Sheep.

EVERY now and again the world is brightened by some man or woman with a soul daring enough to believe that when heaven's Best came down to save earth's

Mrs. Maud Ballington Booth.

worst it was intended that we should follow this example in our own lives.

One of the heroines of this diviner sort who is helping to sweeten the sorrow of our own time is Mrs. Maud Ballington Booth. Mrs. Booth is a connoisseur, so to speak, of "black sheep." If there are any so bad that they are unlovable to the multitude of good people, and forgotten and neglected because of their sins, Mrs. Booth is likely to seek them out, with a soul overflowing with delight at the chance to do them good. Instead of giving up as hopeless the prisoners in our jails and penitentiaries she, inspired by the optimism of Jesus Christ, has set herself not only to carry the Gospel to them while in prison, but to establish homes where they may find a few days of Christian sympathy after their release and from which they may go with kindly encouragement and hope to some honest employment.

On May 24, 1896, Mrs. Booth held a meeting in Sing Sing, giving one of her heart-warming talks, and at the after-service asked those who desired to seek salvation to rise to their feet. Over fifty responded to this appeal. Among those who rose was a young

German, who was deeply touched, and resolved to lead a clean life in the future. It
was some two months afterward that he
was released from prison and came direct to
New York city. He had a little money,
which he had earned while in prison, and
he determined that he would look for work,
and after starting in life afresh would come
to Mrs. Booth and show her how he had ful-
filled his promise. He went to Jersey City
and succeeded in getting employment. At
the end of two weeks, when he received his
pay, he invested all his money in such articles of clothing as he needed, leaving barely
enough to live on during the following week.
But when he went to work on Monday he
found that on account of "hard times" he
was to be laid off. This was a great disap-
pointment. He searched for work for many
weeks, living on almost nothing, still keeping up a brave heart and being honest, until
he got down to his last cent and was a
pauper in the streets. Of course he thought
of Mrs. Booth, "his friend," but, as he told
her afterward, he could not make up his

2

mind to come to her after he had gotten so
low. For days he tramped the streets, sleep-
ing on the wharves and steering clear of the
police, and at last one night started down
the Bowery, hardly knowing what took him
there. He had not gone very far when he
came to the Volunteers' Bowery Post, in the
window of which was a picture emblematic
of " Hope." This picture represents a man
in stripes sitting in his prison cell, with a
look of despair on his face, while in the
background stand two angels, one personat-
ing " Hope " and the other " Love." The
moment his eye rested on the picture he
recognized it, and said, "That is Mrs. Booth's
picture." He gazed at it for a while, and
all the words that Mrs. Booth had spoken in
the prison chapel came back to him—how
they must always feel that she was their
friend. He made up his mind to go and
see her. The following morning he went to
the headquarters of the Volunteers, told his
story, and had a talk with Mrs. Booth.
" Hope Hall " (Mrs. Booth's home for dis-
charged prisoners) was not then formally

opened, but he, being a painter, was set to work painting its interior. He worked faithfully, and shortly after, when officers were sent to take charge of the Home, was converted and has led a beautiful Christian life ever since. He is now regularly employed in a first-class position in New York city. When he went out to seek his present employment he went with a good recommendation from Mrs. Booth. After having been gone for some little time he returned to the office, where Captain Hughes, Mrs. Booth's private secretary, was sitting at her desk. The young lady asked him if he had been successful, yet such a question was scarcely necessary. He grasped her hand, and said, "O, yes; I've got work!" She immediately asked him what his wages were, and, with a happy laugh, he answered, "Why, Captain, I was so glad to get the work I did not stop to ask."

III.

Capturing a Lawyer.

A FEW years since, when a pastor in Boston, Mass., I became very much interested in a young man who was just finishing his

Rev. Wm. N. Brewster.

theological course in the Boston University. The young fellow was so enthusiastic, so optimistic, so bubbling over with faith in God and love for men, and so sure that God was stronger than the devil, that it was a delight to have fellowship with him. When his theological course was completed he went to Cincinnati, to begin his ministry in a plain little chapel in one of the suburbs of that city. There were few members in his little church, and all of them were poor. The outlook would have been very unpromising to many young college men, but to my friend the difficulties in the way only inspired him to greater exertion. I shall never forget the first letter I had from him after he reached the field. It ran like this:

"MY DEAR FRIEND:

"I am on the ground at last, and am beginning to get the lay of the land. It seems good after being in school so long to feel that at last you are on the track and have a fair chance at the race. I imagine that I feel like a hound that has been chafing in his kennel for a long time and is at last turned loose, with the game in sight. The ministry never seemed so precious and splen-

did to me as now, and, by the help of God,
I am determined to win victory for my
Master. I have been looking over my field
here, and am strangely impressed that my
success in getting a strong hold on this community depends on my capturing for the
Lord the most prominent man there is in this
part of the city. The most widely-known
man here, and the man of most influence, is
Judge ——, a distinguished lawyer of Cincinnati. Indeed, he is the most famous
criminal lawyer in this part of the country.
He has the reputation of being a hardened,
sinful man, and there is not the slightest
evidence to show that he has a thought of
becoming a Christian. Yet I feel that I must
win him, and do it at once. You may think
I am foolish about this, and I am astonished
at myself, but, after all, God is as willing to
save him as he is to save anyone else, and I
believe he is as willing to help me secure
this man's conversion as he was to help Paul
and Silas with the jailer at Philippi. Any-
how, I am in for this one thing, day and
night, and scarcely think of anything else.

"Pray for me as you never did before, for
this means everything to me. If God gives
me this man in answer to my work and
prayer at the very beginning of my ministry,

I shall feel that everything is possible after that."

This letter impressed me deeply. The holy audacity of the man amazed me, and I awaited future developments with most prayerful interest.

About ten days later I received a second letter, in which were these lines:

" I could stand it no longer, and so have been to see Judge ——. I just opened my heart and told him all about it. I told him I could hardly sleep or eat on his account, but was praying for him all the time. Everything I intended to say went out of my head, and I just blundered on, trying to tell him how much he owed the Lord and what a great chance there was for him to change the whole community by swinging about and giving his heart to Christ.

" He was the most astonished-looking man I ever saw. He looked at me at first like you have seen a great St. Bernard dog look at a young puppy that runs up to him on the street. Still, he was not offended, but treated me kindly, and I believe God will give him to me yet."

What a battle royal for a human soul! On one hand, the most successful criminal lawyer of the Ohio River Valley—a middle-aged man, hedged about by evil associations and chained by evil habits—on the other hand this ruddy young David with his sling.

I did not hear from the battlefield again for three or four weeks, and was becoming anxious, when one morning I received a letter which began:

" ' Thanks be to God who giveth us the victory through our Lord Jesus Christ!' Judge —— sent for me to come and pray with him last night. He was under deep conviction, and was mourning over his sins. He told me he had not had a moment's rest since the day I first came to see him and told him I was praying for him. I prayed over him and cried over him, and I believe he is happily converted to the Lord Jesus Christ. He will make a public confession in the church, and he and his wife will at once unite with it. What a glorious day that will be for this community! My joy is beyond words. I never can believe anything too hard for God again."

Judge —— became a power for good, and was influential on many a platform in giving his testimony for Christ.

I am sure you will not be astonished after this incident to know that this heroic youth is one of the most successful evangelistic missionaries in China, where, in the populous Hing-hua district, Rev. William N. Brewster has led literally hundreds of the natives to the foot of the cross.

IV.
Elizabeth Stuart Phelps's First Speech.

ELIZABETH STUART PHELPS—or at least that was her name before the " Burglar " had moved " Paradise "— who has led many of us along the glorified

Elizabeth Stuart Phelps Ward.

path between the " Gates " and filled us with a noble ambition to lead " A Singular Life," has put the reading world under a new debt of gratitude by publishing, through magazine and book, some *Chapters from a Life*, and that life her own.

One of the most interesting sketches tells of a day when she was riding through the streets of Gloucester, where "The Old Maid's Paradise" was established, when, noting an excited throng of angry men and women, she inquired of two women talking together at the street side what had happened.

The women looked at her rather scornfully at first, and one made answer: "Haven't you heard? Why, it happened in ——'s rumshop." After a moment's pause the woman continued: "There's a man murdered there. He's just dead. Him and this other feller had words, and he drove a knife into him and out again three times. He's stone dead, layin' there on the floor. See the men folks crowdin' 'round to look at him! If men folks will do such things, they must expect such things to happen. I hope they won't leave stick nor stone to that place, come mornin'!"

" Was he a married man? "

" She lives up the block. And the young ones."

" How many? "

" Twelve."

" Has anybody been to see this poor creature—the widow? Has any woman gone to her? "

" Hey? (Staring.) I guess not. Not that I know of."

Elizabeth Stuart Phelps drove straight to the house where the poor, grief-stricken woman was wailing in the midst of her children. After doing all that she could to comfort her she went back home with a new conception of the horrors that are caused by the liquor traffic. She says herself of this transformation: " All my traditions went down and my common sense and human heart came up. From that day ' I asked no questions, I had no replies,' but gave my sympathy without paltry hesitation to the work done by the women of America for the salvation of men endangered or ruined by the liquor habit."

After thinking the matter over she came to a conclusion most astonishing to all her friends—that she would go on the next Sunday and hold services in the rumshop where the man had been murdered. All their protestations fell on deaf ears, for she had made up her mind, and nothing could turn her from the new path of duty Providence had seemed to make clear.

She visited the rumseller, and he was more than willing to have her use his saloon, for he hoped in that way that something of the shadow of disgrace which hung over his place might be lifted away.

"You'll say, won't you," pleaded the dealer in death, "that this ain't my fault? You'll tell 'em it might have happened anywhere, won't you? Why, it might have happened in a church—there's murders do! You'll say so, won't you, ma'am?"

She did not commit herself as to what the substance of her discourse would be, but secured the services of a lovely, gray-haired Christian woman to assist her. Her heart came near failing her at the last, and she begged her helper to speak in her place. The old lady gently but firmly refused.

Miss Phelps pleaded with her: " I never opened my mouth in a public place in my life. I shall drop of stage fright—and think of the scene !"

When the hour arrived the saloon was packed, and the overflowing crowd extended out into the street. A few women came with her to sing, but most of the hearers were the kind of men who ordinarily frequented this saloon and others like it. The great red stain in the floor, where the man was murdered, was covered from sight by the crowd.

They sang a hymn or two, the new temperance lecturer read a little from the Bible, and then spoke the earnest words that were in her heart, and came away. " Those men listened to us," says Mrs. Ward, " as if they had never heard a message of mercy before in all their lives and never might again. I remember that some of them hung their heads upon their breasts like guilty children, and that they looked ashamed and sorry.

But most of them met us in the eye, and drank what we said thirstily."

That was her first speech, but not her last. For this good work went on for three years, and many a poor tempted man came to bless the woman who had such a strange power over him and his fellows. Often she was accosted on the street by strange men, who would detain her respectfully to say: " I hear when you talk to folks they stop drinkin'. I wish you'd talk to me!"

V.

The Peacemaker's Blessing.

ONE of the sweetest of "the blessings" in the Sermon on the Mount is the one which declares "Blessed are the peace-

Dr. William I. Fee.

makers: for they shall be called the children of God." There is living in Ohio a minister of the gospel of peace whose whole life has been one long work of peacemaking, not only between sinful souls and their God, but between man and his fellow. It would perhaps be no exaggeration to say that for the past fifty years the most successful pastor in winning souls in the Ohio River Valley is Rev. Dr. William I. Fee, whose name is full of fragrance throughout large parts of Kentucky, West Virginia, and Ohio. For considerably over half a century he has been constantly preaching the Gospel, and God has given him wonderful revivals every year.

He has been one of the most modest and retiring of men through it all, but has at last been persuaded to publish a volume, entitled *Bringing the Sheaves*, in which are gathered many striking incidents of his noble and useful life. But turning away from many stories more notable in some ways, I have found this picture of the peacemaker to be very charming in my own eyes:

There was a local preacher and a class leader who had disagreed about some trivial

3

matter.   For years they did not fellowship
with each other.   Their friends became in-
volved in their quarrel, and the entire circuit
suffered in consequence.   Several efforts
had been made to settle the difficulty, but in
vain.   Dr. Fee saw that nothing could so
insure the success of their revival efforts
at the annual camp meeting on which they
were entering as the making of peace between these brethren.   So getting them together on the camp ground, he said, "Let us
go to the woods."

When they reached a secluded place he
asked them to kneel with him in prayer, and
he prayed earnestly that this difficulty might
be settled and they again become friends.
He told them of the injury which was being
done by this unfortunate affair, and the fearful responsibility which was upon them.
He said to the local preacher, "Brother W.,
will you state this case, just as you understand it, as fairly as possible?"

He did so in a very candid manner.

Addressing his opponent, Dr. Fee said,
"Brother P., will you state your case fairly,

just as you understand it, with your matters of grievance, whatever they may be?"

He, with equal fairness, presented his case.

"Now," said Dr. Fee, pleasantly, "I ask each of you one question. Brother W., do you believe Brother P. to be an honest, truthful man, and that he would not willfully tell a falsehood?"

He said, "I do."

"Brother P., do you believe Brother W. is an honest man, and that he would not tell, willfully, a known falsehood?"

Said he, "I believe he would not."

Then said Dr. Fee, "Brother W., you have stated your grievances; Brother P. has stated his. You have agreed to regard each other as honest and truthful men. If this be true, is there anything between you which ought to keep you apart, and which will justify you in involving almost an entire church in a personal difficulty?"

They both said with some hesitancy, "There is not."

"Are you mutually willing, before God,

to settle this difficulty here and now to the best of your ability?"

Each of them replied, " We are."

Dr. Fee said, " Let us pray."

They kneeled down where they were, on the leaves which covered the earth. The doctor prayed, and then asked Brother W. to pray. After clearing his throat a good while, he began. His prayer was not very fervent. Then he called on Brother P., and he had but little spirit of prayer. But this persistent peacemaker did not give up, but after praying again himself, called on each of them, one after the other, to pray again. They did so, and were melted into tears. They arose.

" Now, brethren," said the doctor, " suppose you shake hands with each other and bury this difficulty forever."

Brother W. extended his hand to Brother P., who received it, but each of them looked away from the other. Said the doctor, " That will never do! Look each other in the face, and, with a 'God bless you!' give each other a hearty shake."

They did so, and in a little while their arms were around each other and they were wonderfully blessed. When they returned to the camp ground there was great rejoicing among the people. This reconciliation was the beginning of a glorious revival.

VI.

Tunneling for a Soul.

T has been my privilege to ride in a railway train through the four greatest tunnels in the world: the Mullin tunnel, on the Northern Pacific Railroad in Montana; the Hoosac tunnel in Massachusetts; through Mt. Cenis tunnel in Italy; and, greatest of all, through that marvel of engineering which hurls a train sheer through the St. Gothard Alps, with six thousand feet of snow and ice above it.

But an infinitely more interesting and significant tunnel than either of these is the tunnel from Helen Keller's finger tips, along the line of her nerve, back into the brain and heart that only a few years ago were imprisoned in an Egypt-like darkness.

Not long since, on opening a daily paper, I saw a series of headlines that caused the tears to run down my cheeks, so profoundly were my emotions stirred. The headlines announced that Helen Keller had, the day before, virtually passed the preliminary examination for entrance to Radcliffe College, in Cambridge, Mass. Perhaps I felt more keenly on the subject because of the fact that I was living in South Boston when Helen Keller first came there from Alabama for training under the protection of the Perkins Institution for the Blind, and had been from the first deeply interested in the brave and self-denying efforts put forth to rescue her from her lonely bondage.

Young people who have all their senses, and yet have found their preparation for college fraught with difficulties sufficient to test their best energy and endurance, will stand appalled before one who only a few years ago was wrapped about by a double-walled prison. Think of it! Eyes and ears both closed. Two of the ordinary windows of life shut up and closely blinded. Only one possible means of communication, and that the nerve in the finger tip. Back along that nerve went the patient, persevering effort of the teacher, knocking at the cell door of an imprisoned soul. There was a soul there well worth tunneling for. With en-

Helen Keller.

From a photograph by A. Marshall, Boston.

thusiasm and gladness it awoke to the new knowledge and liberty that were offered it.

And now, a few years later, so heroically has this liberated soul set herself to work to conquer all obstacles that we have a young girl whose acquirements would be more than brilliant if no window of the soul had ever been closed against her.

If she is near enough to anyone to put her delicate finger tips on the lips, she receives with accuracy everything spoken to her, and replies in beautiful language and in softly modulated tones, the sounds of which she herself never hears.

She reaches forth after all knowledge possible for mortals to know. She is tireless in her explorations, and gives promise of an intellectual triumph that shall be the marvel of our time. Surely, all things considered, hers is the palm for heroism among all the young women of the present generation.

Edmund Clarence Stedman sings a beautiful ode to Helen Keller:

> Mute, sightless visitant,
>   From what uncharted world
>   Hast voyaged into life's wide sea
> With guidance scant?
>   As if some bark mysteriously
>   Should hither glide with spars aslant
>   And sails all furled.

But Helen Keller has not been willing to leave the sails furled; she has aroused herself to meet every breeze that offered, until, in spite of all obstacles, she is entering her young womanhood with all sails spread to the winds of life.

The Christian religion, with its love and trust and hope, has come to Helen Keller's mind and heart as naturally as the love of mother or friends. To great-souled Phillips Brooks was granted the rare privilege, a few years since, of answering the questions of her inquiring mind in regard to spiritual things. The correspondence, which was published at the time, was one of great interest.

If it is a matter of so much importance to carry the light of intelligence and love into one human mind and heart that have been shut about by imprisoning walls, how grand is the opportunity of the Christian Church to carry the Bible, and the civilization that follows in its wake, to the millions in heathen lands who are shut in by the dark walls of their ignorance and superstition!

VII.

The Pilot's Conversion.

THERE is no more interesting character about any of our great seaboard cities than the ocean pilot. He goes out with every passenger steamer, and the last fond

Captain Josiah Johnson.

notes and postal cards sent back to the loved ones left behind are committed to his care.

When he drops over the deck's side into his little boat, and waves his grave farewell, all on board feel that they have cut loose from home and are committed for weal or woe to the mysterious paths of the sea.

No one is so earnestly looked for by both captain and passengers on an incoming steamship as the pilot, who brings with him news from the great busy world, from communication with which the steamer has for many days and nights been cut off. He is the forerunner and prophecy of the harbor not yet in sight; an assurance that the voyage is over, its dangers are passed, and the desired haven will be soon at hand.

Of all the pilots on the Atlantic coast the Sandy Hook pilots are of most interest, because of the multitude of ships that come and go to and from New York Harbor. There are among the Sandy Hook pilots two men who began their apprenticeship over a half a century ago, in 1846. One of these is Captain Josiah Johnson, of Brooklyn, who, after five years' apprenticeship, was licensed a pilot in 1851, and has been in constant service, going and coming past Sandy Hook, for forty-six years.

Captain Johnson came to the sea by inheritance, as his father served on the old frigate *Constitution* in the War of 1812. In spite of his long term of service he carries his sixty-five years with the air of a victor, and his great, stalwart frame and bronzed face and sturdy step are wonderfully youthful, although his hair and beard are white as snow.

This veteran pilot has, naturally, in his half-century of service, been in many a gale and faced bitter storms. Three men in as many awful hours of danger have been swept overboard from the deck by his side to their death. Many a schooner, disabled, his pilot-boat has rescued from the teeth of the storm, and captain and crew and owner have owed life and property to his skill and courage. Numerous have been the wrecks from which, in the nick of time, he has taken the sailor who had lost hope and expected to perish. Many a time Captain Johnson and his crew on their pilot-boat have been out

for days in the bitter cold of a winter's
storm, until their clothing was sheathed in
ice, so that when they were at last permitted
to remove it, it would stand upright like an
iron frame. Yet on such nights and in such
storms he has hailed hundreds of ships and
guided them safely into the harbor without
the loss of a single charge committed to his
care in his lifetime of service.

My acquaintance with Captain Johnson,
however, did not begin upon the sea, but in
an evangelistic service in Brooklyn held under the leadership of Dr. J. Wilbur Chapman, of Philadelphia. I noticed a large,
fine-looking man sitting in the audience,
and watched the eagerness with which he
seemed to listen to the Gospel message,
and was not surprised when the invitation
to seek Christ was given that his strong
hand was uplifted. Later, in the inquiry
room, I had the privilege of conversation
with him, and saw how, with the simplic-
ity of a little child, he yielded his heart
to the Saviour, and was most happily converted. It was one of the greatest joys of

the meetings, after that, to watch the captain's broad, weather-beaten face, which beamed with "a light that never was on sea or land," as he listened to the gracious offers of mercy and the rich promises of God's word.

One night he came to me at the close of the evening service and told me that he would have to go the next day, on his pilot-boat, to meet an incoming vessel, and so would be absent from the meetings. As he grasped my hand to say good-bye his eyes filled with happy tears, and he exclaimed: "It will be the happiest trip I have ever made past Sandy Hook; for this will be the first time that the Great Pilot will be consciously present with me."

Thank God, we may all have the Great Pilot with us!

"Slacken no sail, brother,
   At inlet or island,
Straight by the compass steer,
   Straight for the highland.

"Set thy sail carefully,
   Darkness is round thee,
Steer thy course steadily,
   Quicksands may ground thee.

" Fear not the darkness,
    Dread not the night,
God's word is thy compass,
    Christ is thy light.

"Crowd all thy canvas on !
    Out through the foam !
It soon will be morning
    And heaven be thy home."

VIII.

The Mother of "Ben Hur."

ONE of the most queenly of living women to-day is Mrs. Zerelda G. Wallace, of Indiana, the widow of ex-Governor David Wallace, of that State, and the noble woman whose fidelity as a stepmother— giving more than a mother's usual devotion and tenderness—reared Lew Wallace to be a distinguished general in the War of the Rebellion, afterward Minister to Turkey, and, greater than all, to have the qualities of mind and heart that could produce *Ben Hur*. This noble woman not only reared to honorable fame her three stepsons, but also six children of her own, and grandchildren have kept her heart young in later years. She exemplifies the "new woman" who is yet to bless the world—a woman so large-minded and broad-hearted as to keep a constant interest in public affairs without in any way losing the gentleness and refinement of her womanhood.

4

It is said of Mrs. Wallace that when her husband became governor of his State she, by virtue of her position and her rare men-

Mrs. Zerelda G. Wallace.

tal qualities, might have been what is known as a " leader " in social circles, but her soul was too great to be satisfied with the little round of social ceremonies and vanities; she

cared for society only as she found in it men
and women of grand ideas and heroic purpose.   Her husband was a man of fine literary culture, and together they enjoyed
every new book, every speech or sermon,
that came in their way.   In this way their
evenings at home were almost ideal in their
domestic beauty.   When the babies were
put to bed Governor Wallace would read to
her the latest political speech or newest book,
which they would discuss with the zest of
professional critics.   Everything Governor
Wallace wrote—speech, essay, or argument
—was submitted to her for criticism or
approval.   Though she knew nothing of
equity as taught in the books, he complimented her by saying that her unerring
sense of justice at once lighted upon any de-
fect or discrepancy in jurisprudence, while
her fine literary taste was invaluable in regard to rhetorical symmetry.   As her stepsons grew older she read law with them.
In that way she not only kept in splendid
fellowship with their young hearts, but became one of the best educated women in the

science of jurisprudence in the country.
Such a home picture realizes Tennyson's
poetic vision :

> Two heads in council; two beside the hearth;
> Two in the tangled business of the world;
> Two in the liberal offices of life;
> Two plummets dropped for one to sound the abyss
> Of science and the secrets of the mind.
> In the long years liker must they grow;
> The man be more of woman, she of man.
> He gain in moral height, nor lose
> The wrestling thews that throw the world.
> She, mental breadth, nor fail in childward care,
> Till at the last she set herself to him
> Like perfect music unto noblest words;
> Then comes the statelier Eden back to man,
> Then reigns the world's great bridals, chaste and
>   calm,
> Then springs the crowning race of human kind.

Mrs. Wallace is, as we would expect, a
woman of the largest charity and forbearance. Frances Willard relates that when,
in 1874, the Crusade clans gathered in Cleveland for the organization of the Woman's
Christian Temperance Union, Mrs. Wallace
was nominated as chairman of the Committee on Resolutions. Miss Willard, not
yet knowing Mrs. Wallace, moved that the
name of Mother Stewart, who had been so

closely identified with the Crusade, should
be substituted in her place. Immediately
after Miss Willard went to Mrs. Wallace,
to whom she had never spoken as yet, to
explain her action. That great-hearted
woman grasped her hand warmly, and
said, "When you know me better, my
friend, you will discover that in this sacred
cause I have lost sight of all personal con-
siderations." What a magnanimous and chiv-
alrous heart was disclosed in that utterance!

One of the most splendid tributes ever
given to any woman was paid to Mrs. Wallace by her stepson, General Lew Wallace,
on the occasion of their first meeting after
his immortal book, *Ben Hur*, had been published. He asked her for her opinion on the
book.

She replied, "O, my son, it is a nonesuch
of a story, but how did you ever invent that
magnificent character, the Mother?"

"Why, you dear, simple heart," he answered, with a kiss, "how could you fail to
know that the original of that picture is
your own blessed self?"

IX.
Diaz—The Apostle of Cuba.

ONE of the most heroic souls that has come to the front in connection with the Cuban insurrection against Spain is Diaz, the devoted Baptist minister, who, by his unflagging energy, marvelous self-sacrifice, and splendid ability as a preacher, has gathered about him in the city of Havana a church of nearly twenty-five hundred members and a congregation of eight thousand souls.

In Clarendon Street Baptist Church, Boston, about six years ago, he told the story of his conversion and the development of his work as a minister. When he was converted he immediately commenced his labors in his own family. They were astonished and troubled to hear him talking of Christ, the Bible, and salvation, and were greatly opposed to it, his mother refusing to listen to him. Every member of the family was against him, with the exception of a little

four-year-old sister, who, after hearing of
Christ, said, "I like that man, and will love
him."   His mother was a Roman Catholic,

Dr. Alberto J. Diaz.

and very bitter against what he said.   She
called him a Protestant, a heretic, a Jew.
She said, "I will not speak to you if you do
not come back to the church and the religion
I taught you."   He tried to tell her about

Christ and his word, but she would not listen to him; all she would say was, "If you are my son and love me, you will leave that religion and come back to the Catholic Church." She knew very well that he loved her, and what she said troubled him greatly. She would not speak to him, though they lived in the same house, for months. He trusted in the Lord, however, and prayed constantly for her conversion.

He was very much surprised one evening to see her come in and take a seat in the meeting. Her presence disturbed him, as he thought she had come to reprove him before the people, but, mastering his feelings, he preached his usual sermon and then gave the invitation to those who wished to become members to stand up. His mother was one of the four who arose. Now, he thought, surely she intended to speak to him. Three of the people stood on his right; his mother was on his left. Not knowing what she would do, he turned and began to examine the other three, hoping she would keep silent and go away.

He was thus intently engaged when one of the people said, "Mr. Diaz, there is your mother standing over there; why don't you speak to her?"

Turning to her, he said, "Well, mother, what are you doing here?"

"Alberto," said she, "don't you want me in your church?"

"Yes, mother, we want you if you are ready to receive the Lord Jesus Christ; but how is it that you have changed?" he asked, in great surprise.

"Through the Lord Jesus Christ, whom I have found in your Bible?" she answered.

Then she turned to the people and told of the trouble they had had; how she had not spoken to her son for so long a time, but when she had read her Bible and found the way to salvation she could no longer resist coming and joining them.

Diaz says: "When my mother was in my own hands, and I was about to immerse her, all the words that my tongue would give utterance to were, 'Lord Jesus, this is my mother; have mercy.'"

After his mother came to the light his greatest anxiety was for the conversion of his father. He was a man of science, who, absorbed in his studies, thought, like many others, that religion was something good enough for women and children, but nothing for a man to have anything to do with.

The son approached him one day with the Bible and said, "Father, don't you want to read this book?"

"No," said he, "that book is too old. I want something new."

Talking with his mother about it, she asked, "Do you think, Alberto, that if father reads the Bible, he will be converted?"

"Yes," said the young preacher; "if we can only get him to read the Bible, he will soon be converted."

"Then I will make him read the Bible," she exclaimed. So in about three or four days, when Sunday came, she went to him. "Father, won't you please read those three or four verses for me? I am in a great hurry, and I want to know my lesson before I go to Sunday school," she said.

The old scientist was very devoted to his wife, and so he took her Bible and read the verses she had pointed out to him. Under various pretexts she kept him reading the Bible for her. Early one morning, a little while later, young Diaz awoke, and seeing a light in the next room, thought some one was sick, and going to see what was the matter, was so surprised that he could not speak. There sat his father reading the Bible at four o'clock in the morning. He said to him, "Father, what have you been doing here?"

"O, I have been reading this book," he answered; "what time is it?"

"Four o'clock," replied the young man.

"Four o'clock! No; it cannot be more than eleven."

But the surprised and delighted son told him it was really four o'clock, and asked how he liked the book.

"I like this book," said the old man, "and will go with you next Sunday."

He went to the church on the following Sunday, was happily converted to Christ, and entered upon a joyous Christian life.

X.

The Heroine of Alaska.

FIFTEEN years ago I was on board a train on what was then the only railroad in western Washington, making

Mrs. A. R. McFarland.

the journey from Portland, Ore., to the new and straggling village which has since grown into the ambitious young city of Tacoma. It was a slow train, for the roadbed was new, but the tedious hours lost their weariness to me after making the acquaintance of one of my fellow-passengers who was on her way back to Alaska to take up her mission work among the Indians.

My new acquaintance was Mrs. A. R. McFarland, who had gone to Alaska four years earlier and devoted herself to the saving of the young girls in that far-off land. For more than a year this lady, delicately reared and cultured, fitted to enjoy the refinements of society, was the only white woman in Alaska Territory, because she believed it to be her duty and esteemed it her privilege to teach her ignorant heathen sisters of the North the truths of that Gospel which has lifted the burden from woman's shoulders in every land where it has been carried. I shall never forget the thrill of admiration and reverence that went through my heart as I listened to her story. I felt myself to be in the presence of one of the world's purest and bravest spirits.

Mrs. McFarland was not only for a long time the only white woman in that vast and lawless region, but she was for many months the only Protestant missionary in Alaska. In those days the people brought all their troubles to her for solution. If they were sick, they came to her as a physician; if death came to the wigwam, she was called upon to take charge of the funeral. When there was a quarrel in the family, and husbands and wives were estranged, she was the peacemaker to settle their difficulties and bring harmony again to the distracted family circle. In their simple property troubles she was often judge, lawyer, and jury. When feuds sprang up among the small tribes she became peacemaker on a larger scale and arbiter of their differences. When the Christian Indians called a constitutional convention they paid a noble tribute to her goodness and wisdom by electing her chairman. She was often called upon to interfere in cases of witchcraft; and when the vigilance committee among the miners decided to hang a white man for murder

she was sent for to act as his spiritual ad-
viser. Her fame followed the coast line to
the different tribes, and every canoe carried
some note of praise for the missionary.
Great chiefs left their homes and came long
distances that they might enter the school
of " the woman that loved their people."

Mrs. McFarland soon found, to her horror, that the intelligence and blessing which
her school, with its teaching and hope,
brought to the girls only put them in
greater peril by making them more attractive to the wicked and lawless white men who
inhabited the Alaskan towns. Among a
people where heathenism crushes out a
mother's love and makes her willing to sell
her own daughter, soul and body, for a few
blankets or a canoe load of provisions, she
found that her brightest and most promising
pupils were in the greatest danger. As they
improved their advantages in the mission
school it manifested itself in their external
appearance. They began to comb their hair
more smoothly, to dress more neatly, and to
pay more attention to cleanliness in their

person; their dull, heavy countenances began to light up with intelligence; and as
their attractions increased white men were
the more anxious to buy them for base pur-
poses. Again and again Mrs. McFarland
had to interfere to save her schoolgirls from
lives of sin. This necessity was the cause
of her establishing an industrial training
school for Indian girls, where they lived together in a " Home," into which she gathered such promising girls as were in danger
of being sold, and trained them up to be
the future Christian teachers, wives, and
mothers of their people.

The story of how she secured her first
girl for the " Home " illustrates the fearful
odds against which she had to contend and
the splendid heroism of her character.
Katy, one of the schoolgirls, fourteen years
of age, who had attended her mission school
from the commencement, was about to be
taken up the river and sold to the miners by
her mother. Mrs. McFarland, hearing of
it, started to visit the family, who lived on
an island. When she reached the point

where she usually crossed the tide was so
high she could not get over. By signs she
attracted Katy's attention, who came across
in a canoe. She was sent back for her
mother, who came over. There for an hour
and a half, seated on a rock by the shore, in
a pouring rain, Mrs. McFarland pleaded
with the heathen mother until she promised
not to take Katy away. But the next week
the mother broke her promise and tried to
compel her daughter to accompany her to
the mines. The canoe was prepared and
the mother took her seat; the blankets, provisions, and younger children were in their
places, but the little girl lingered on the
shore, crying and begging most piteously.
Finally, when they would have put her in
by force, she straightened herself up and
said, " Mother, you may kill me, but I will
not go with you and live a life of sin." She
then ran into the woods and hid. When
her mother had gone she came out and
claimed Mrs. McFarland's protection. And
that was the way the first " Girls' Home "
in Alaska was started.

5

XI.

The Heroism of Forbearance.

WE are accustomed to think of the hero as one who achieves his victories by some positive and aggressive action. It is often, however, as heroic to remain silent under unjust attack as it is to speak in the face of opposition. There is a heroism that bears as well as a heroism that performs. David, on returning from one of his military expeditions, declared that the heroism of those who remained behind to care for the baggage was as deserving as that of those who went forth to battle, and in the division of the spoils decided. "As his part is that goeth down to the battle, so shall his part be that tarrieth by the stuff."

An incident which occurred in the young manhood of Dr. George Lansing Taylor, the well-known preacher-poet, illustrates this important phase of Christian heroism. Dr. Taylor was growing up through boyhood into manhood in Ohio when he became

a Christian and joined the church, and, like
many another, had to suffer from his school-
mates. The indignities were hard to bear,

Dr. George Lansing Taylor.

but he acquired at the very outset of his religious experience a spirit of brotherly love,
even for those who abused him.

One day he was sharpening a pencil, when
a book slipped off the desk and fell upon

the floor. He bent over to pick it up, with
his large sharp jackknife open in his hand.
The boy who was his chief persecutor gave
his hand a kick which drove the knife into
it, gashing it fearfully. He shut his hand
so tightly as to stop the flow of blood.
Then, rising, with no sign of anything having gone wrong, he asked permission to go
out. Crossing the street to the house of the
nearest doctor, he had the wound sewed up
and dressed.

The surgeon was very indignant. "Do
you know," said he, "you have come within
danger of losing the use of your right hand?
Who was it that kicked you? You can make
him smart for it. His father can be made
to pay well for such a job as that. Who
did it?"

But the plucky young fellow refused to
tell. He was far more anxious to do the
boy good than to have him suffer for his
meanness. And, though he had only to
mention his name to insure his being se-
verely punished and probably expelled, he
never showed by word or look that he re-

sented the injury. The love of Christ had taken all resentment out of his soul.

Six or seven years later he had finished his college course and had taken the principalship of a school for the training of teachers. Among his pupils was the young man, though older than himself, who had kicked the knife into his hand. The result of young Taylor's heroic forbearance had proved the wisdom of Paul's advice in his letter to the Romans: "Avenge not yourselves, but rather give place unto wrath : for it is written, Vengeance is mine; I will repay, saith the Lord. Therefore if thine enemy hunger, feed him; if he thirst, give him drink : for in so doing thou shalt heap coals of fire on his head." This old-time enemy was now a most devoted friend; not one of the scholars was more faultlessly loyal than the man who had once treated him so cruelly, but who had been conquered by his forbearance.

After a time there was a great revival of religion among the pupils of the school, and many of them were converted. One afternoon this same young man asked Dr. Taylor

if he might talk with him a few minutes,
and when they were alone he inquired:

"Do you remember the time when I
nearly ruined your right hand by a brutal
kick?"

Dr. Taylor replied that he remembered
the occasion very well.

"I had no idea of hurting you so badly,"
he continued, "but I hated you because you
had become a Christian. You never seemed
to resent it in the least, and now I want to
tell you that that jackknife has been sticking in my heart ever since. Lately the Lord
has been twisting it around until the agony
has become unbearable. I want you to forgive me and ask God to help me out of this
torment about my meanness."

And there alone together teacher and
pupil mingled their prayers at the mercy
seat, and the years of remorse were ended
and an era of joy and peace came to the
young man's soul. From that hour the two
young men were brothers in the sweetest
friendship. How rich the reward of his gentleness and forbearance!

XII.
Struggling Genius.

THE most interesting personality that hovers about the famous old forest and palace of Fontainebleau, in France, is

Rosa Bonheur, the Famous Artist.

by no means to be selected from the ghosts of the dead and historic past; to many peo-

ple it is rather the very live and vigorous
Rosa Bonheur, who dwells* at the estate of
By, near the village of Moret.

Rosa Bonheur passed her childhood in the
midst of the most exciting scenes. Her
little sister was born while the cannon were
booming in the Revolution of 1830. Just
before the door of her father's house the
Royal Guards mounted a piece of artillery,
which fired on the Place de la Bastille. The
little Rosa came very near being a victim of
the Revolution. Her father had climbed up,
and was standing on the inner bolt of the
door, in order to peer through the transom
at the fight which was going on outside.
When the cannon was fired the shock of the
explosion shook the door violently, throwing
him from his position, and he barely escaped
crushing the child to death in his fall.

For years after this the times were very
hard with the painter's family. Her father
had no work, and, in 1852, to make matters
worse, the cholera broke out. One of the
memories of this remarkable woman, that
she shudders even now to recall, is a vision

of carts upon carts, filled with dead bodies, following one after another all day long.

Her mother died when she was still but a little girl and left her in distressing loneliness. She began to paint very early, and while her father was hunting everywhere through the city of Paris for students to whom he could give drawing lessons she worked alone as best she could in a little studio in the garret. One night when her father returned home after his day's labor he found her finishing her first oil painting after nature—a handful of cherries. " Why, that's fine," he said, "and in future you must work seriously."

Her love for animals was early developed, and she would wander through the outskirts of Paris, among the fields and farms and dairies, making studies of cows, sheep, and goats. Finally, she found a delightful little corner of wild scenery near one of the parks, and went and boarded for several months with an honest old peasant woman. It is interesting and encouraging to every struggling young person to know that Rosa Bonheur's genius by no means relieved her of the drudgery of the beginner in any great art. Day after day she studied the rapid movements of animals, eagerly watching the shimmer of their coloring in the sun. She learned that each cow or horse or dog has an individuality of its own as much as has a human being, and formed the habit of making separate studies of each animal.

The first picture she exhibited in the Salon was in 1845, and was a modest little canvas representing rabbits. Two years later she won a gold medal. When the young girl appeared before the Director of Fine Arts, who, with many pleasant compliments, handed her the medal in the name of the king, she, to his great surprise and intense amusement, replied, " Thank the king very much for me, and deign to add that I intend to do better next time."

In 1893 the distinguished Duc d'Aumale, whose sad death the whole world regretted as one of the tragic results of the terrible fire in the Paris Charity Bazar, invited Rosa Bonheur to be his guest at Chantilly, the famous estate which the public-spirited duke willed to the people of that land which had honored him in his youth and exiled him in manhood. The famous painter of "The Horse Fair" took with her her first poor little medal, stamped with the effigy of Louis Philippe, the Duc d'Aumale's father. The duke was greatly pleased, and smilingly remarked, "It brought you good luck."

In addition to her undoubted genius, inherited from her father, Rosa Bonheur owes her marvelous success to that patient, honest, plodding study which she conscientiously gives to all her work, and that unsatisfied spirit which is suggested in her answer to the Director of Fine Arts, in her girlhood, "I intend to do better next time!" The world is better for Rosa Bonheur.

XIII.
Kindling the Gospel Fire in a Northern Wigwam.

ONE of the most magnetic men with whom it has ever been my privilege to converse is Rev. Egerton Ryerson Young, the famous missionary to the Indians of British Columbia. Mr. Young is one of those dauntless souls who would win success and fame in almost any department of life. There is no such word as fail in his vocabulary. When he undertook to carry the Gospel to the Indians in their lonely wigwams in the northern woods he put into the work the same inventive genius, indomitable purpose, and tireless fidelity that other men have put into the building of railroads and managing of armies and nations. But back of his strong brain and immense energy there is a heart full of love for Christ and tender sympathy for the poor people to whom he carried the glad news of salvation.

Mr. Young has the art of recounting his

experiences with a peculiar breeziness pertaining to the woods where they were encountered. One of his best stories is of a long

Rev. Egerton Ryerson Young.

journey which he made into the heart of the wilderness in search of a tribe which he had not visited before. He made this trip in a canoe paddled by two Christian Indians. When they reached the forest encampment their welcome was not very cordial. The

Indians were soured and saddened; a great
many of their children having died with
scarlet fever, which had been brought into
their land, for the first time, by some white
traders the year before. With the exception
of an old conjurer or two, none openly opposed him, but the sullen apathy of the
people made it very discouraging work to try
to preach or teach. However, he did the
best he could, and was resolved that, having
come so far and suffered so many hardships
to reach them, he would faithfully deliver
the message, and leave the results to Him
who had permitted him to be the first to visit
that land to tell the story of redeeming love.

One cold, rainy day a large number of the
people were crowded into the largest wigwam
for a talk about the truths in the great Book.

Mr. Young's faithful Christian canoeists
aided him all they could by giving personal
testimony to the blessedness of the great salvation; but all seemed in vain. The company sat and smoked in sullen indifference.
When questioned as to their wishes and pur-
poses all he could get from them was, "As

our fathers lived and died so will we."
Tired out and sad at heart, the missionary
sat down in quiet communion and breathed
a prayer for guidance and help in this sore
perplexity. In his extremity the needed
assistance came so consciously that he almost
exulted in the assurance of victory. Spring-
ing up, he shouted out: "I know where all
your children are who are not among the
living! I know, yes, I do most certainly,
where all the children are whom death has
taken in his cold grasp from among us, the
children of the good and of the bad, of the
whites and of the Indians; I know where all
the children are!"

Great, indeed, was the excitement among
them. Some of them had their faces well
shrouded in their blankets as they sat like
upright mummies in the crowded wigwam.
But when he uttered these words they
quickly uncovered their faces and manifested the most intense interest. Seeing that
he had at length got their attention, he went
on: " Yes, I know where all the children are.
They have gone from your camp fires and

wigwams. The hammocks are empty and
the little bows and arrows lie idle. Many of
your hearts are sad, as you mourn for these
little ones, whose voices you hear not, and
who come not at your call. I am so glad
that the Great Spirit gives me authority to
tell you that you may meet your children
again, and be happy with them forever. But
you must listen to his words which I bring
to you from his great Book, and give him
your hearts, and love and serve him. There
is only one way to that beautiful land, where
Jesus, the Son of the Great Spirit, has gone,
and into which he takes all the children who
have died; and now that you have heard his
message and seen his Book you, too, must
come this way if you would be happy and
enter therein."

While he was thus speaking a big, stalwart Indian from the other side of the tent
sprang up and rushed toward him. Beating
on his breast, he said: "Missionary, my
hearty is empty, and I mourn much, for none
of my children are left among the living;
very lonely is my wigwam. I long to see

my children again, and to clasp them in my
arms. Tell me, missionary, what must I do
to please the Great Spirit, that I may get to
that beautiful land, that I may meet my
children again?" Then he sank upon the
ground at Mr. Young's feet, his eyes overflowing with tears, and was quickly joined
by others, who, like him, were broken down
with grief, and were anxious now for religious instruction. To the blessed Book they
went, and after reading what Jesus had said
about little children, and giving them some
glimpses of his great love for them, Mr.
Young told them "the old, old story," as
simply and lovingly as he could. There was
no more scoffing or indifference. It was the
beginning of a blessed work which resulted
in the winning of nearly the entire tribe to
a happy experience of the saving love of
Christ.

6

XIV.

The Heroine of the White Ribbon.

I SHALL never forget my first glimpse of Frances Willard, the renowned leader of the white ribbon hosts. She was making

Miss Frances E. Willard.

a tour of the Northwest in company with Miss Anna Gordon, her inseparable other self. She had come to Portland to attend a

convention, and as I was then pastor at Vancouver, Wash., seven miles away, on the
other side of the Columbia River. I determined, if possible, to secure her for a meeting
the following Sunday night. I wrote her
that if she would come, I would secure the
largest hall in the place, and do such preliminary work as would insure the organization of a local Woman's Christian Temperance Union. She replied that she had to
speak at Portland on Sunday morning, but
if I would meet them with a carriage on
Sunday afternoon, they would come to Vancouver and hold the meeting.

Vancouver was at that time, as it is now,
the military headquarters of the Department
of the Columbia, and General Nelson A.
Miles, now at the head of the United States
Army, was in command. I was on good
terms with Colonel Morrow, who was in
command of the local fort at Vancouver,
and on applying to him secured a government ambulance, four splendid great mules,
with a uniformed driver and guard of state
for the occasion. And so on that summer

Sunday afternoon, fifteen years ago, those four mules and the government ambulance appeared before Miss Willard's astonished gaze as she sat awaiting us on the piazza of a friend's house in Portland.

I do not believe Miss Willard will ever forget that ride. It was very dusty and hot, and the old ambulance, though a very formidable piece of roadway furniture, was anything but an easy carriage to ride in. The driver was on his mettle and bent upon showing off his mules, and the time we made across the peninsula between the Willamette and the Columbia Rivers was a caution. Miss Willard and Miss Gordon adapted themselves to the situation and took it all in good part, but I think they were exceedingly amused at the whole performance.

The meeting was a great success. The largest hall in the town was packed to the last person that could find standing room. General Miles presided with great dignity; Colonel Morrow, Captain Henry Pierce, and other army officers, with their wives, and distinguished citizens crowded the platform,

Thurston Daniels, since lieutenant governor
of the State, was one of the ushers.

Miss Willard was at her best. I have
heard her many times since, and always
with admiration, but never when her play-
ful wit, marvelous pathos, and persuasive
logic seemed to hold the audience with a
more profound spell than it did that night.
At the close of her address a vigorous
Woman's Christian Temperance Union of
more than sixty members was organized,
and both Miss Willard and Miss Gordon
felt amply repaid for the hot, dusty, and
uncomfortable ride in the government ambulance that Sunday afternoon.

One of the secrets of Miss Willard's remarkable success is her willingness to adapt
herself to the situation of the hour, and do
whatever needs to be done at once at whatever personal cost.   This spirit is illustrated
in her work in behalf of the Armenians.
While the prime ministers and diplomats of
half a dozen nations were standing about
fumbling their fingers and trying to per-
suade the Sultan to be good and stop perse-

cuting the Armenians—the murders going on all the while—Miss Willard and her stanch friend, Lady Henry Somerset, set themselves to work to do the deed of sisterly kindness that was in their reach. They went to Marseilles, where hundreds of fugitive Armenians were landing from every Eastern ship, and set up a restaurant to feed these hungry brothers and sisters. Theirs were the first hands stretched out to help the despairing immigrants as they landed on European soil. Theirs were the sympathizing faces into which the hopeless travelers looked, and hoped and took courage again. No wonder their restaurant soon came to be known as " The Kitchen of Jesus Christ."

XV.

The Apostle to the Red Men.

DR. CUYLER says that Bishop Westcott, of Durham, England, once said to Miss Smiley, "The most apostolic man I ever met is your Bishop Whipple." A good many of us believe that Englishman to be a good judge of an apostle.

Bishop Whipple has been the life-long friend of the American Indian. At the first missionary meeting which he attended after his consecration as a bishop one of the older bishops said to him: "You are to speak to-night; don't say anything about Indian missions—they are a failure. You are a young bishop and cannot afford to be thought an enthusiast." Little did that conservative bishop know the character of the man with whom he was dealing. When Bishop Whipple came to speak he took the audience into his confidence and frankly repeated the advice that had been given him, and, taking that for his text, he proceeded to deliver a warm-hearted appeal for sending the Gospel to the red men.

He never tires of telling stories of the Indians, among whom he has preached so

Bishop Whipple.

long. Once, when he had distinguished visitors at one of his missions, the Indians prepared a pantomime for the entertainment of the bishop and his friends. The chief,

Wah-a-bouquot, asked him: "Does your English friend know the history of the Ojibways? Would he like to hear it?" On receiving an affirmative answer he continued: "Before the white man came the woods and prairies were full of game, the lakes and rivers were full of fish, and the wild rice was the Great Spirit's gift to the red man. I will show you some of my people as they were before the white man came."

The door of the house opened, and out came an Indian dressed in skins and ornamented with colored porcupine quills, and by his side an Indian woman in a neat dress of skins trimmed with fur.

The chief said: "My father, you see the Indians such as they were before the white man came. Shall I tell you what the white man did for us? He said: 'You have no houses, no firehorses, no firecanoes, no books, no implements of toil; give us your land and we will make your people as the white man.' The white man had a forked tongue. I will show you what he gave us."

Then came out a man with face be-
smeared with mud, in a ragged blanket,
without leggings, and by his side an Indian
woman in a tattered calico dress. The
chief cried: " O God, is this an Indian?
How came it? " The Indian took out from
under his blanket a black bottle and said,
" *Iskotu-wabo* (fire-water); the white man
gave it to us."

The chief then said: " Many moons ago
a pale white man came to see us. We hated
white men and would not listen. But each
year when the sun was so high we knew we
should see that white man coming through
the pines. We called a council. We asked:
' Why does he come? He does not trade.
He asks nothing from us; perhaps the Great
Spirit sent him.' We did listen and took
that story to our hearts. Shall I tell you
what it has done for us? "

Then came out of the house an Indian in
a black frock coat, and by his side an Indian
woman in a black alpaca dress. The chief
said, " My friends, there is the only religion in the world that can lift a man out of

the mire and tell him to call the Great Spirit
his Father."

A skeptical traveler who was present
grasped Bishop Whipple by the hand and
exclaimed, " All the arguments I have read
in defense of Christianity are not equal to
what I have seen to-day ! "

XVI.

Up to Heaven on Wings of Song.

MARY A. LIVERMORE is one of the few of those splendid personalities who accomplished service of national interest and importance a generation ago, but have gone on with ever-increasing enthusiasm and freshness of spirit into the new world of to-day. Mrs. Livermore threw her sublime energy, immense store of practical wisdom, and boundless tenderness of heart into caring for the sick and wounded sol-

Mrs. Mary A. Livermore.

diers during the dark days of the War of the Rebellion. In her thrilling book, *My Story of the War*, there is, perhaps, gathered more heart-stirring incidents than are found in any other volume which has grown out of that historic period.

Here is one which reveals some of the

characteristics of this great-hearted, heroic woman :

She was one day nearing the completion of her tour of a hospital ward, when she paused beside the cot of a poor fellow on whose face the unmistakable look of death was settling.

" You are suffering a great deal," she said.

" O yes! O yes!" he gasped; " I am, I am; but not in body. I can bear that. I don't mind pain—I can bear anything—but I can't die! I can't die!"

" Why are you afraid to die?" she in- quired. " Tell me, my poor boy."

" I ain't fit to die. I have lived an awful life, and I'm afraid to die. I shall go to hell."

She drew a camp stool to his bedside, and, sitting down, put her hands on his shoul- ders, and spoke in commanding tones, as to an excited child, " Stop screaming. Be quiet. If you must die, die like a man, and not like a coward. Be still, and listen to me." And she proceeded to combat his fear of death and his sense of guilt with assurances of God's willingness to pardon. She told him of Christ's mission on earth, and assured him that however great had been his sins they would be forgiven of God, since he was penitent and sought forgiveness. She bade him repeat after her the words of a prayer, which he did with tearful earnestness. She strengthened her assurances by Bible quotations and illustrations from the life of Christ, but she felt she was making little impression on the dying man. At last the poor fellow exclaimed, "Can't you get a minister? I used to belong to the church, but I fell away. O, send for a minister!"

Mrs. Livermore was determined that nothing should be left undone that might bring comfort and salvation to the poor fellow, and, on inquiry, found that the hospital steward was also a minister, and soon had him at the man's bedside. To him the wounded soldier listened eagerly. After the steward had talked with him a little, and prayed with him, Mrs. Livermore inquired, "Can't you sing?"

Immediately, in a rich, full, clear tenor, whose melody floated through the ward and charmed every groan and wail into silence, the steward sang hymn after hymn, all of them familiar:

> "Come, humble sinner, in whose breast
>   A thousand thoughts revolve.
>
> " Love divine, all love excelling,
>   Joy of heaven, to earth come down.
>
>   " Jesus, Lover of my soul,
>   Let me to thy bosom fly.
>
>   " My days are gliding swiftly by,
>   And I, a pilgrim stranger."

All of these hymns were so well known to the dying soldier that she saw he followed the singer, verse after verse. The music affected him as she had hoped. The burden rolled from the poor boy's heart, and, in feeble, tender tones, he said: " It's all right with me, chaplain! I will trust in Christ! God will forgive me! I can die now! "

" Sing on, chaplain! " Mrs. Livermore suggested, as he seemed about to pause to make reply. " God is sending peace and light into the troubled soul of this poor

boy through these divine hymns and your
heavenly voice.   Sing on; don't stop!"

He continued to sing, but now chose a
different style of hymn and tune, and burst
forth into a most rapturous strain :

> " Come, sing to me of heaven,
> For I'm about to die ;
> Sing songs of holy ecstasy,
> To waft my soul on high.
>
> " There'll be no sorrow there,
> There'll be no sorrow there.
> In heaven above, where all is love,
> There'll be no sorrow there."

She looked down the ward and saw that
the wan faces of the men, contracted with
pain, were brightening.   She looked at the
dying man beside her and saw, underneath
the deepening pallor of death, an almost
radiant gleam.

Then the chaplain was summoned away
by a call from his office.   It was getting late
in the afternoon, for she had tarried a
couple of hours at this bedside, and her
friends came from other wards of the hospital to say that it was time to return.

" Don't go; stay!" whispered the fast-sinking man. The words of the Master rushed to her memory, "Inasmuch as ye have done it unto one of the least of these, ye have done it unto me," and she promised to remain with him to the end. The end came sooner than anyone thought. Before the sun went down, with courageous heart and rapturous face, he had put out to sea for the immortal shore.

7

XVII.

On the Edge of a Crevasse.

NANSEN, the Arctic hero of the hour, has almost every element that is adapted to arouse the admiration and enthusiasm of those who love the strong, the daring, and heroic in mankind.

He is a man of splendid stature, and trained as he has been from his childhood to all the virtues of the athlete, he is one of the most rugged and tireless specimens of physical manhood the world affords to-day. He has succeeded where other men failed, not only because of his dauntless courage, but because nature and training have fitted him to perform feats of physical endurance that few men in the world could accomplish.

Once, on his arrival in London, he mingled in a great crowd at Buckingham Palace, and pushed himself up to the front just as the Princess of Wales arrived to hold a drawing-room. As he was waving his hat with the crowd in honor of the princess he

Dr. Fridtjof Nansen.

felt a twitch at his watch chain and knew that
he was being plied by a pickpocket. But
Nansen had altogether too cool a head to let
such a little thing excite him, as would have
been the case with a smaller man; he simply
dropped his left hand and let its giant-like
grip grasp the wrist of the thief. Without
even looking to see who it was he continued
to cheer and wave his hat aloft in his right
hand until the enthusiasm had subsided.
Then he quietly handed his prisoner over
to a policeman. Nansen said he merely
held the man tightly, but the miserable
wretch was howling with pain, and declared
that he would rather go to prison than have
his bones crushed.

On one occasion, when returning to camp
after an absence, they saw their canoes drifting from land with all their provisions and
necessaries of life. To reach the boats was
a matter of life or death. Not to reach them
was certain death. The great qualities of
the explorer came out quick as a lightning
flash, when, without a moment's hesitation,
he sprang into the ice-cold water and swam

after the drifting canoes. He was chilled to the bone, but he succeeded in his object, and brought the canoes safely back to camp.

It was no group of weaklings that Nansen had with him, either. One incident reminds us of the story of David. On one occasion, while dragging their sledges along a narrow patch, they were suddenly confronted by a polar bear, but Johansen, a fit companion for Nansen, caught the great beast by the throat and held him at arm's length, while his chief sent a bullet through his heart with his rifle.

Perhaps no twitter of birds ever fell more sweetly on human ears than those which Nansen describes in *The First Crossing of Greenland*. As they were breakfasting in their walled tent in the midst of the ice desert of the desolate North, they were astonished to hear, as they thought, the twittering of a bird outside; but the sound soon stopped, and they were not at all certain of its reality. But as they were starting again after their one o'clock dinner that day they suddenly became aware of twitterings in the air, and,

as they stopped, sure enough they saw a
snow bunting come flying after them. It
wandered around them two or three times,
and plainly showed signs of a wish to sit
upon one of their sledges. But the necessary audacity was not forthcoming, and it
settled on the snow in front for a few moments before it finally flew away with another encouraging twitter.

Very welcome indeed was that little bird,
for it gave them a friendly greeting from the
land they were sure must now be near. Nansen says, "We blessed it for its cheering song,
and with warmer hearts and renewed strength
we confidently went on our way." How
many such snow buntings of hope God sends
to cheer and warm the hearts of those who
face hardship and peril with unshaken in-
trepidity and courageous purpose!

But even in sight of land they came near
losing their lives. As the wind came up
very strong in the afternoon they sought to
travel more rapidly by setting sail on their
sledges and using them as iceboats. Their
ships flew over the waves and drifts of snow

with a speed that almost took their breath
away.   After a time, as it was growing dusk,
Dr. Nansen ran ahead of the sledges on his
snowshoes to make sure that they should not
come to any sudden disaster.   His prudence
saved their lives, for, as they were rushing
along through the dense driving snow, he
suddenly saw, in the general obscurity,
something dark lying right in their path.
He took it for an ordinary irregularity in
the snow, and unconcernedly steered straight
ahead.   The next moment, however, he
found that they were on the edge of a chasm
broad enough to swallow sledges, steersman,
and passengers.   A single moment later and
they would have forever disappeared, and
have been more completely lost to the world
than was the fated Dr. Franklin.

XVIII.

Saint Content Wintergreen.

CONTENT WINTERGREEN has come to her sainthood through what most people would call great tribulation, though she

Saint Content Wintergreen.

herself never thinks of it as such, and does not dream that anything she has done would look heroic in the eyes of anyone.

Content Wintergreen was born seventy-nine years ago in a little town in Central New York. When she was still a child her mother died, and her father brought his family of three girls and a boy to try their fortunes in the then small city of Brooklyn. Sixty years ago Content Wintergreen found the source of all true contentment in a sweet fellowship with Jesus Christ.

The family were poor, and the girls early sought to help bear the burdens of the household by working in a tailor's shop or bringing their work home, as Content did after a while, when the father was ill. One of the sisters married and went away to enjoy the happiness of her own home and family, but as the other sister soon lost her health, Content had no time to think of love affairs, save to care for the loved ones of her own household. The brother had grown up and gone West, and on Content's frail shoulders fell all the burden of the home.

The father died soon afterward, and though that wrung her heart, she had not time for morbid grief, for there was her in-

valid sister to provide for still. For fourteen years she wrought with her needle and
earned enough to care for them both, and
ministered with a mother's love and tenderness to her sick companion, who was never
able to go beyond the door of their humble
room.

During the last and most trying year of
her sister's illness a letter came from the
brother telling the sad news that he had been
stricken by a fatal disease and longed to come
home and die in the arms of some one who
loved him. There was not a moment's
hesitation. Content thought only of the
blue-eyed brother who had been the play-
mate of her childhood, and in a most loving
letter she bade him come. This made three
months to feed instead of two, and a double
burden of nursing; yet in recounting this
experience she says, "Those were very
happy days, after all. Though we were poor,
we loved each other and were so happy together." The brother after a few months
passed away, and only a little later the sister,
too, faded out of life.

"The only time I was ever tempted to murmur," said Content, with a wistful face —and I knew by the far-away look in her eyes that a picture of other days was passing before her inner vision—"was when my sister died. It was hard, the working all day and the being up so much nursing her in the night, but love made it light, and I had cared for her so long that I think I felt about her as a mother does for a crippled child."

During all these years of toil and nursing Content Wintergreen never for a moment thought of excusing herself from Christian work. For forty years she was one of the most persevering and successful tract distributors that Brooklyn has ever known. She could not go to church much, and seldom had time to seek out anyone for a personal talk, but she never allowed herself to go out of the room to the tailor's shop, or to the grocer's, or to the market, without her little bundle of tracts, which with gentleness and skill she gave out here and there with a kindly word of good cheer that made them

welcome. Many a home among the poor
was sweetened by the little visitor carried
into it from the market-place. In this way
Content Wintergreen introduced her divine
Lord and Master, whom she loved so well
and served so faithfully, to hundreds of
people.

For a long time now Content has lived
alone, and on her next birthday she will have
reached her fourscore years. She is not able
to work much, and a kind relative pays her
room rent, and allows her four dollars a
month for living expenses; out of that four
dollars she provides her provision and fuel
and clothing.

Her constant theme is the goodness and
mercy of God, and the abundance of his
blessings to her. Her desire to be a worker
for Christ is as strong as ever. A young
friend who had been for a long time taking
her the newspapers to read, on one occasion,
desiring a paper in which to wrap a parcel,
said to her: "Auntie Wintergreen, what be-
comes of all the papers I bring? You never
seem to have any about here." The dear

old saint flushed red like a schoolgirl caught whispering, and stammered out: " I hope you won't mind, but I save the papers up, and every two weeks I take them down to the jail. I thought I might perhaps do a little good yet in that way."

Her face is wrinkled and worn, but her soul is flushed with immortal youth, and in the resurrection glory it will glow forever with the peace of Him whom having not seen she loves.

XIX.

The Father of Prohibition.

ONE evening, many years ago, a woman came to the home of Neal Dow, in Portland, Me., in great distress. She was the wife of an intelligent, capable citizen, with a large, promising family. He held a government position, and executed the duties of his office to the great satisfaction of the department and of the public; but he had one terrible habit, which grieved and mortified his family and friends and threatened the loss of his office: it was periodical intemperance. On his way back and forth from his office to his house he passed a certain liquor saloon, and was enticed into it.

On this occasion the wife was in great sorrow and fear. She said her husband had been away from his desk and was now in this saloon; that if he did not at once return to his employment, he would be removed from office, and the family would be left in shame and destitution.

The veteran Neal Dow in his home at Portland, Me.

Neal Dow went immediately to the saloon and inquired for his neighbor. At first the rumseller endeavored to conceal his customer, but Mr. Dow found him and requested the proprietor to sell him no more liquor.

He replied, " I must supply my customers."

" But, don't you see," said Mr. Dow, " that this gentleman has a large family to support? If he neglects to go to his office to-morrow, he will lose his place. I beg of you do not sell him any more strong drink."

The rumseller then grew angry and said he, too, had a family to support; that he had a license, and would sell to all who called for it, and that he wanted none of Dow's advice.

Neal Dow's answer was : " So you have a license, and support your family by the impoverishment and ruin of other families? With God's help I will try to change all this! "

How he did change it all, how he sowed Maine knee-deep in temperance literature,

how he traveled and spoke and argued and
conquered, the whole world knows. But it
is doubtful if the present generation of
younger people has much conception of the
eloquence of which this man was capable
half a century ago. Mr. George H. Shirley,
at present a citizen of Brooklyn, and one of
Mr. Dow's faithful coadjutors in that great
campaign, says of him: " Many times have
we heard him pour forth the most scathing
invectives and the most brilliant utterances
against the traffic, and not hesitating to de-
nounce the rumseller by name. These oratorical efforts were equal to the best speeches
of Sumner or Phillips. I have often been
surprised that he escaped physical injury
from his opponents."

The secret of Dow's great success was his
utter fearlessness and his readiness to attack
the wrong wherever he found it, and his
keen feeling of personal responsibility for
every evil it was in his power to right. The
following incident sets forth this chief heroic characteristic of the man:

Neal Dow was once passing down one of
8

the streets of Portland, when he noticed a crowd of people, among whom was the mayor of the city. In the center of the group was a country lad crying. The lad had been imposed upon by a noted horse jockey of the town, who had got the boy drunk and then induced him to swap the horse he had driven into town for an old plug. Upon hearing his story, telling the boy to follow him with the jockey's horse, Mr. Dow led the way to the latter's stable, nearly a mile distant. Not finding the jockey in, the old horse was turned into the stable and Mr. Dow, with the country lad still following, started back to town. On the way they met the jockey. He was driving in a wagon to which the lad's horse was attached.

" That's my horse," said the boy.

Mr. Dow stepped into the road, took the horse by the bridle, and, calling to one of his employees who happened to be passing at the time, told him to unharness the horse, which he did, the irate jockey, meanwhile, threatening to take the law on Mr. Dow, who replied, " You will always know where to find me."

Then, telling the boy to take the horse, he started again for the city, where the lad's wagon had been left.

" Look a-here," said the jockey, as they went, " what am I to do with my wagon? "

" Do what you like," said Mr. Dow.   " It is nothing to me."

As may be expected, the country lad was full of joy and profuse with thanks.   When he had harnessed his horse he said to Mr. Dow, " Now, what can I do for you? "

" Promise me not to drink any more." And the boy did so.

Some three years afterward Neal Dow was stopped by a countryman in the streets, who, with mouth stretched on a broad grin, said, pointing to a horse, " There he is.   I hain't drunk no more."

XX.
" The Good-luck House."

ABOUT eighteen years ago Mrs. Alice N. Lincoln, a young lady of high culture and refinement, with means at her com-

Mrs. Alice N. Lincoln.

mand to live a life of ease and indifference to the world's sorrows if she had so pleased, became very deeply interested in the pitia-

ble condition of many of the poorer people
in the tenement houses of Boston, and undertook with heroic determination to do what
was within her power to better their condition.

She hired a large house in the heart of
Slumdom. It contained twenty-seven tenements, and she paid one thousand dollars a
year rent for the first year and afterward
twelve hundred. The house had a bad reputation, morally, and had been for some
time under the ban of the police. At the
time she took it half the tenements were
empty, because of the degraded character of
the occupants. Its entries and corridors
were blackened with smoke; the sinks were
in dark corners, and were foul and disease-
breeding; the stairways were innocent of
water or broom, and throughout the entire
house from top to bottom everything was
dirty and neglected. It was surely not an
attractive task to attempt to bring cleanliness and order out of such chaos, but this
resolute young reformer deliberately set herself to perform the seemingly impossible.

The interior was painted; an improved
method of lighting and ventilating the sinks
was introduced; fresh plaster replaced the
moldy wall paper in the entries, and wood
and coal closets were provided for each tenement on its own landing. Previously all
the fuel had been kept in the cellar. A few
of the worst tenants had to be removed, but
the majority, pleased with the new order of
things, were willing to accept the rules and
remain. Tenants were soon found for every
room; and this house, which had been a
hive for fevers under the old *régime* of
greed, that did not care how dirty the tenants were so long as they paid their rent,
became, under the new rule of cleanliness,
so healthy that disease was almost unknown,
and was, and is to this day, known by the
tenants and the neighborhood generally as
" The Good-luck House."

During all these years Mrs. Lincoln has
collected her own rents, and kept everything
well under her own supervision. A close account of all receipts and expenditures has
been kept. At the end of the first year the

balance of cash in hand was $111.67, or more
than eleven per cent on the investment. The
second year it was still more profitable, the net
sum at the end of the year being $157.47.
Mrs. Lincoln still carries on the administra-
tion of "The Good-luck House," and no
queen was ever treated with more genuine respect than she is there. She is regarded as a
most practical sort of patron saint to the institution. Yet there is no element of charity suggested in her dealings with her
tenants.. It is simply Christian justice. With
great care she seeks to help them retain
their self-respect, and treats them as fully
her equal in personal responsibility. The
rent is required to be paid regularly. One
rigid rule enforced upon all tenants is cleanliness. She pays for the weekly scrubbing
of the halls and stairways, but the tenants
are required to sweep them every day in
turn. The sinks and drains are kept clean.
All this has a marvelous effect on the home
habits of the inmates; and I have seen as
clean and tidy rooms in "The Good-luck"
tenement house as I have seen anywhere,

and that, too, on days when they were caught unawares, it not being the regular rent day.   .

Mrs. Lincoln has a conscience, and justly feels that if six per cent interest is enough for business men to pay on money borrowed, it is enough for poor people to pay on their investments in rents, and so all the profits above six per cent she puts into the bank as an emergency fund, and from time to time the tenants have been permitted to share some unexpected pleasure from this surplus.

XXI.

Sheldon Jackson's Night on the Deep.

ONE of the most heroic personalities of modern times, and one who might fitly be included in any group of heroic spirits in any age of the world, is Rev. Sheldon Jackson, D.D., who, in a higher sense than any ecclesiastical power could designate, is the Bishop of all Alaska. Dr. Jackson has indeed been a father to the forgotten and neglected tribes of that far-away Arctic wonderland. He has not only traveled thousands of miles, and endured loneliness and hardship to carry the Gospel to the natives in their heathenism, but he has been ever ready to thrust his persistent and invincible personality between these poor ignorant creatures and the cruel and rapacious human sharks who would prey upon them. He has also been indefatigable in his self-denying efforts to introduce the reindeer into their impoverished land and secure them from extinction by starvation.

Dr. Jackson's whole career in Alaska is one heroic story, but here is a simple account of one little missionary trip in a canoe

Rev. Sheldon Jackson, D.D.

which, for motive, exposure, and danger, might well be put alongside of Paul's trip when he was shipwrecked on his way to Rome:

At three o'clock in the morning they were aroused, and were soon under way without any breakfast. This did not matter much, however, as their entire stock of provisions consisted of a limited quantity of ship biscuit and smoked salmon—biscuit and salmon for breakfast, salmon and biscuit for dinner, and straight salmon for a change for supper in the evening. The Indians upon the trip only averaged one meal in twenty-four hours. As they were passing the mouth of a shallow mountain stream the canoe was anchored to a big rock. The Indians, wading up the stream, in a few minutes with poles and paddles clubbed to death some thirty salmon, averaging twenty-five pounds each in weight. These were thrown into the canoe and taken along.

At noon they put ashore for their first meal that day. Fires were made under the shelter of a great rock. The fish, cleaned and hung upon sticks, were soon broiling before the fire. After dinner all hands took a nap upon the beach.

At three in the afternoon they were again under way. When night came the Indians could find no suitable landing-place, and

paddled on until two o'clock next morning,
having made a day's work of twenty-three
hours. Finding a sheltered bay, they then
ran ashore. As it was raining hard, they
spread their blankets as best they could under sheltering rocks or projecting roots of
the great pines.

After a few hours of uncomfortable sleep
they again embarked. Toward evening
they passed Cape Fox and boldly launched
out to cross the arm of the sea, and once out
they found the sea becoming so rough that
it was as dangerous to turn back as to go
forward. The night was dark, the waves
rolling high, and the storm beating upon
them. One Indian stood upon the prow of
the canoe all night, watching the waves and
giving orders. Every man was at his place,
and the stroke of the paddles kept time with
the measured song of the leader, causing
the canoe to mount each wave with two
strokes; then, with a click, each paddle
would at the same instant strike the side of
the canoe and remain motionless, gathering
strength for the next wave. As the billows

struck the canoe it quivered from stem to stern.

In the morning they landed at an old deserted Indian village, whose forest of totem poles told of the heathenish rites and superstitions from which he was trying to save this wretched people. These horrid monuments of the past with their grinning faces spoke to him only too plainly of savage butcheries, horrible cannibal feasts, inhuman torture of witches, and fiendish carousals around the burning dead.

The Indians were so exhausted by the labors of the past night that they were compelled to go ashore and get some rest. On shore they tried to start a fire, but the driving rain soon extinguished it. Taking his regulation meal of salmon and hard tack, Dr. Jackson spread his blankets under a big log and tried to sleep. The beating storm soon saturated the blankets, and he awoke to find the water running down his back. Rising, he paced up and down the beach until the Indians were ready to move on. After a rest of two hours, seeing no sign of a lull in the storm, they reembarked on their journey.

Such journeys this heroic man was willing to take that he might carry the Gospel to his brethren whom he had never seen before, and who had no more claim on him than they have upon us. And yet how hard it is for us sometimes to carry a message of hope and salvation to the neighbor of our own color and tongue who has become disheartened and is perhaps perishing for just the word of good cheer we can speak. Thinking of Jackson's dark night in the canoe, may we be inspired to go on our errand for the Master this very day!

XXII.

The First March of the Woman's Temperance Crusade.

A BOY of sixteen, the son of Judge Thompson, of Hillsboro, O., came home one night after listening to a lecture on temperance by Dr. Dio Lewis, of Boston. Finding his mother still up, he related to her that in the course of his remarks Dr. Lewis had told how his own mother and several of her good Christian friends had united in praying with and for the liquor sellers of his native town until they had given up their soul-destroying business, and then had said, "Ladies, you might do the same thing in Hillsboro if you had the same faith." Afterward he had put the matter to vote, and more than fifty of the women by rising had pledged themselves to make the effort.

"And now, mother," said the enthusiastic boy, "they have got you into business; for you are on a committee to do some work at the Presbyterian church in the morning at

nine o'clock, and then the ladies want you
to go out with them to the saloons."

Judge Thompson had that evening returned from court in another county, and

Mrs. Thompson, of Hillsboro, O.

being very tired, was resting on the sofa.
The mother and son, supposing that he was
asleep, had been talking in an undertone;
but as the boy spoke about his mother going
to the saloons the judge suddenly roused

up and exclaimed, " What tomfoolery is all that?" The boy slipped out of the room and went to bed, while Mrs. Thompson assured her husband that she would not be led into any foolish act by Dio Lewis or anybody else. After he had relaxed into a milder mood, though continuing to scoff at the whole plan as " tomfoolery," she ventured to remind him that the men had been in the " tomfoolery " business a long time, and suggested that it might be " God's will " that the women should now take their part.

The next morning after breakfast, when they were gathered in the sitting-room, the boy came up, and laying his hand on his mother's shoulder, inquired, " Mother, are you not going over to the church this morning?" As she hesitated and doubtless showed in her countenance that she was greatly perplexed, the boy said, " But, my dear mother, you know you have to go." Then her daughter, who was sitting on a stool at her side, leaned over in a most tender manner, and looking up in her face, said, " Don't you think you will go? "

9

During the progress of this conversation
Judge Thompson had been walking the
floor in silence. Suddenly he stopped, and
placing his hand upon the family Bible that
lay upon his wife's work-table, he said,
"Children, you know where your mother
goes to settle all vexed questions. Let us
leave her alone"—going out of the room as
he spoke, the children following him.

Mrs. Thompson turned the key in the lock
and was in the act of kneeling down to pray
when she heard a gentle tap on the door.
Upon opening it she found her daughter
with her Bible open and the tears coursing
down her cheeks as she said, "I opened to
this, mother; it must be for you." She immediately left the room, and her mother sat
down to read with new insight the wonderful message of promise in the 146th Psalm.

Doubting no longer what her duty was,
she at once went to the Presbyterian church,
where quite a congregation had already
gathered. She was at once unanimously
chosen as the president, Mrs. General Mc-
Dowell as vice president, and Mrs. D. K.

Finner as secretary of the unique work which they were to perform. They drew up appeals to druggists, saloon keepers, and hotel proprietors.

Then Dr. McSurely, the Presbyterian minister, who had up to this time occupied the chair, called upon the new president to come forward and take her place. She tried to get up; but having never done any public work, her limbs refused to act, and she sat still. Wise Dr. McSurely looked around at the men and said, " Brethren, I see that the ladies will do nothing while we remain; let us adjourn, leaving this new work with God and the women."

After the men had filed out and the door was closed behind them new strength seemed to come to Mrs. Thompson, and she walked forward to the minister's table, took the large Bible, and, opening it, told the story of the morning in her own home. After she had tearfully read the psalm and commented on it, she called upon Mrs. McDowell to lead in prayer. Now, Mrs. McDowell, though a good Christian woman for

many years, had never in all her life heard
her own voice in prayer; but she prayed that
morning as though Isaiah's "coal of fire"
had unsealed her lips.

As they rose from their knees Mrs.
Thompson asked Mrs. Cowden, the wife of
the Methodist minister, to lead in the singing
of the old hymn, "Give to the winds thy
fears;" and turning to the rest of the women
she said, "As we all join in singing this
hymn let us form in line, two by two, the
small women in front, leaving the tall ones
to bring up the rear, and let us at once pro-
ceed to our sacred mission, trusting alone in
the God of Jacob." As they marched out
through the door of the church into the
street they were singing these prophetic
words:

> " Far, far above thy thought
> His counsels shall appear,
> When fully He the work hath wrought
> That caused thy needless fear."

And thus was begun the first march of
that mighty crusade that proved to be a divine contagion which has spread to the ends
of the earth.

XXIII.

The Hour of Decision.

THERE is one hour forever sacred to every earnest man who has, after the years of childhood, consciously chosen

Dr. Jesse Bowman Young.

Christ for his Saviour and consecrated himself to the service of God.   Many a time on

the frontier in Oregon, at the great camp
meetings held in the leafy groves, I have
listened to the old men and women as with
tearful earnestness, and yet with buoyant,
joyous spirit, they told of that hour of hours
when they broke away from sin and chose
Jesus Christ to be the Captain of their salvation.

I have an hour like that in my own memory that I would not blot out for the price
of worlds. It was one night at a watch-
night service in a little Western college
chapel. It was almost midnight, and the
appeal to let the old year die with all the old
sins, and the new year bring in a new life
of righteous purpose, had been very clear
and strong. The audience were on their
feet singing, and some were going to the
altar in witness of their holy purpose. I
stood at the end of the seat next the aisle
and longed to go, but had not the courage,
until an old carpenter with one leg shorter
than the other, so that he limped painfully
at every step, came down the aisle with the
eye of a fisherman after souls. As he drew

near he laid his hand upon my shoulder and said, "Louis, is it not time for you to go?" The weight of the old man's limp pushed me a step down the aisle, and on I went toward a Christian life. I have always said, "It was the weight of the old man's limp that did it."

It is such a story of decision, only one with far more romantic and heroic surroundings, that I started in to tell.

I have just been reading Jesse Bowman Young's beautiful book, *What a Boy Saw in the Army*, a rare and fascinating sketch of what a boy saw of those weird and terrible days of struggle. It was just before the battle of Gettysburg, and this youth, who had gone to the front, as did many another from both North and South, while only a lad, was lying in the grass in a very sober mood, running his eye along the gathering lines of men, now peering anxiously across the landscape to the westward, noting the woods behind which the Confederates were concentrating their forces and wondering why the battle did not open.

This boy had faced death on the battle-field many a time before, and it was not fear that made him sober. It was God's call to his conscience. Above all other meditations —thoughts of home, of loved ones far away, of the course of the battle—sounded in his soul the question, " What about the future? Suppose you are killed, what will become of you? In a few moments the tempest will break over this field, and you will have to face it. You cannot now escape in any way from this emergency. In the face of the opening battle how about the future? Are you ready to meet God and to face the issues of another world? "

Lying there on the hillside, he was troubled and overwhelmed at the outlook. He had been brought up in a religious home, had been taught to be a Christian from childhood; but amid the roughness, the exposures, the grossness, and the dissipation of army life for nearly two years many of these lessons and early impressions had grown dim, and many of the admonitory voices which had sounded a clear, strong

note at home had ceased to influence him.
Now, in a desperate emergency, with the
possibilities of death before him, his sins
rose up in alarming array, and his neglected
soul was smitten with a sense of its needy
and suppliant condition. " O Lord, have
mercy on me !" was the single cry of his
broken heart as he sought to keep back the
tears, maintain his composure, and hide the
tumult which disturbed his breast. Then
he bethought himself of the Bible he carried, his mother's parting gift, the book
that he had neglected and slighted of late.
Turning to it and catching at it as a drown-
ing man at a straw, he opened it at random.
The leaves parted at the 121st Psalm, and
his eyes fell, as he glanced at the page,
on these words, " The Lord shall preserve
thee from all evil: he shall preserve thy
soul."

The utterance seemed like a direct revelation from the skies. The boy felt as though
there was One who had taken knowledge of
his destitute estate, his fears, his remorse,
his sorrow, his anxiety, his cry for help.

The words got hold of him, and he got hold of the words with a grip that has never ceased from that day to this. The vows made in that hour of danger and trouble were never forgotten. While brooding on the passage so strangely applicable to his time of peril and want his heart was lightened, and at least a part of the burden was rolled away. He had scarcely put up the book and buckled on his sword before all along the line the order ran, " Fall in, men ! " and the battle was on.

Through days of struggle on the battlefield and days of waiting in camp, through a life full of courage as pastor and editor, that one hour in Rev. Dr. Jesse Bowman Young's life has shone the most resplendent of all.

XXIV.

The Heroine of a Leper Colony.

MARY REED was an Ohio school-teacher, and a good one, too. She taught ten years and enjoyed her work, until God's call came to her to carry the good news of Christ and his salvation to her unfortunate sisters in India. The call was so clear that she could not resist it, and so, thirteen years ago, she found herself in charge of zenana work in Cawnpore. She had but fairly become accustomed to her daily service when she was taken very ill and was sent to Pithora, a healthful spot in the Himalayas, for recovery. Only three miles from where she stopped was an asylum for lepers, and her tender heart yearned in sympathy for them when she learned of their pitiful lot. Her health being restored, she went back to Cawnpore, and there and in Gonda put in five years of hard work, coming home to America in 1890, to get her strength again in her mother's home.

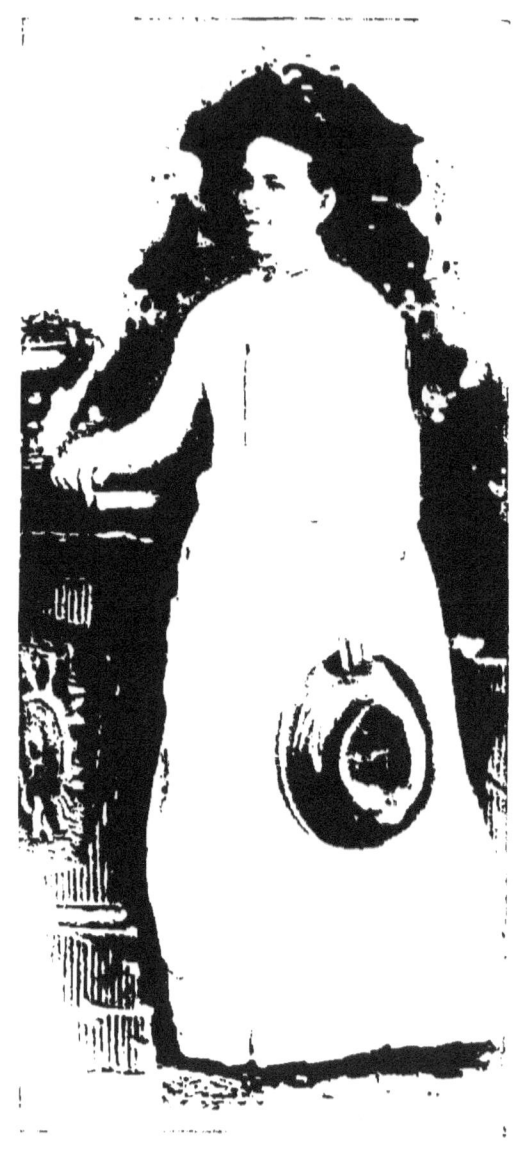

Miss Mary Reed,

While at home she began to suffer from a peculiarly severe pain in her finger. A strange spot also appeared on her cheek, low down near the ear, and one day it came over her like a flash that leprosy had fastened its pitiless fangs in her body. She did not tell her mother, but confided her secret to two or three friends who could assist her in making arrangements to go to that mountain retreat at Pithora as a missionary to the lepers. She bade her mother farewell, knowing it must be farewell forever in this world, and bravely set her face toward the East; in her tenderness not permitting the dear ones at home to know of her disease until she had reached India.

In order that she might be sure of her fate she consulted eminent specialists in London and Bombay, who confirmed her worst fears. She was indeed a leper. But with sublime Christian heroism she went to her destiny not with a sad face, but bravely, with strong confidence and earnest determination to make the very most out of the time that yet remained. A friend who

traveled with her on her journey writes
these beautiful passages:

" Here and there we held sweet hours of
communion, and I, who had been accustomed
to see missionaries seeking America in feeble
condition, could not refrain from asking if
it was right for her to return to India at an
unfavorable season, before her health was
established. Her lips quivered, but her
gentle, pleading voice grew steady as she
replied, ' My Father knows the way I go,
and I am sure it is the right way;' and at
another time she said, ' I am returning to
India under conditions such as no other missionary ever experienced.'

" It was in Paris that she said one evening,
' If I thought it was right, and you would
promise never to speak of it until you heard
it in some other way, I should tell you my
story.' I told her if aught in me inspired
her confidence, that was the surest safeguard
of her secret.

" On memory's walls there will hang
while time lasts for me the picture of that
scene. A wax taper burned dimly on the

table beside her open Bible—that Book of all books, from whose pages she received daily consolation; and while, without, Paris was turning night to day with light and music and wine, within, Mary Reed's gentle voice, faltering only at her mother's name and coming sorrow, told the secret of her affliction.

"As my throbbing heart caught its first glimpse of her meaning I covered my face to shut out the swiftly-rising vision of her future, even to the bitter end, and almost in agony I cried out, ' O, not that! Do not tell me that has come to you!' . . .

" I come with sorrow to my last evening with Miss Reed. I sat in the shadow, and she where the full moon rising over the snowy mountains just touched her pale, sweet face with a glory that loved to linger. Again I hear her voice in song:

    "'Straight to my home above
      I travel calmly on,
    And sing in life or death,
      My Lord, thy will be done.'

" On the shores of lovely Lake Lucerne, hand clasped hand for the last time on earth, and with eyes blinded by gathering tears, our farewells whispered: ' God be with you till we meet again.' "

Miss Reed went directly to the leper asylum at Pithora, and, although for a time the disease made rapid progress, and she suffered a great deal, she bore all without murmuring. Her letters home were full of the sublime confidence and unfading joy of the Christ whose banner she is bearing to victorious conquest among the poor lepers of the Himalayas. Think of the glory of the splendid triumphs of faith in this American girl, ten thousand miles from home, slowly dying from a terrible disease in a leper colony in India, who could write home one August morning sentences like this: " I could not tie myself down to my writing-desk this morning in quietness of heart till I first sat down at my dear organ, and played and sang, with all the thirteen stops out, ' I am dwelling on the mountain where the golden sunlight gleams.' "

What wonder that God has given Mary Reed wonderful evangelistic power among

the lepers under her care, and that there are
constant conversions among those who be-
hold her radiant face, and who breathe the
atmosphere of her joyous self-sacrifice!

10

XXV.

From Slave Kitchen to a College Presidency.

IT seems most fitting that the man who above all others is the leader of the negro race in America, and who appears to have every element of safe and wise leadership, should be called Washington. As George Washington was the father of his country, Booker T. Washington gives great promise of becoming, in a very real sense, the father of his race in industrial freedom in this country.

Vast sums of money have been consecrated by Christian and public-spirited men and women to bring light and hope to the millions of the colored people. In response, thousands of educated youth are coming out of what a generation ago was a race of slaves; but of them all Booker T. Washington is the first who has caught the ear of mankind, and shown himself to have not only the graces of the orator, but the sagacity, the prophetic spirit, and the wisdom of the statesman.

His whole life, from the day of his birth in a log-kitchen, where his mother was cook for the farmhouse, reads like a romance.

Booker T. Washington.

In his boyhood he slept on a pallet on the dirt floor of the kitchen where he was born, and until the close of the war his body was clothed simply in a tow shirt. He declares that the hardest thing he ever had to do on the plantation was to wear that tow shirt. It was made of the roughest part of the flax. The tow was so harsh and jagged that when he put it on it was like having a hundred pins sticking into his chest and back and arms. It took him a full month to get a new shirt broken in.

His first great ambition was born in his heart by seeing a young colored man reading a newspaper to a crowd of his friends, who were listening eagerly and looking at the reader with expressions of awe and reverence. He saw that being able to read gave one a higher position, and he at once wanted to learn the art. It was two years before he had a chance, and that chance would have amounted to nothing except to a hero. He worked all day, and then walked five miles to his teacher's house, and then back home again.

When he was fourteen years of age, and while working in a coal mine, he overheard some talk of General Armstrong's school for colored boys at Hampton, Va. His ambition at once flamed up with the purpose of going to that school. He saved up twelve dollars, and set out for Hampton. He did not know where Hampton was, but, getting the general direction, walked that way. He reached Richmond, Va., without money, without friends, and, having no place to stay at night, he walked the streets until midnight, and then, being quite worn out, crept under a sidewalk and slept till morning.

This would have discouraged most boys, but heroes like Booker Washington are not easily discouraged. The next morning he hired out to work on a ship that was unloading pig-iron. He worked on this ship through the day, and slept under the sidewalk at night, till he had earned money enough to reach Hampton, where he arrived with fifty cents in his pocket.

He applied at once to General Armstrong for an opportunity to work his way through the school. That great man sent him to the lady principal. She gave him a room to sweep. He swept it and dusted it three times in order to make sure of an entrance into the school. Pretty soon the principal came in, and, putting her finger on the wall and looking in the cracks, said, "I guess you'll do for janitor."

At those words the young man's heart leaped for joy. He took care of four or five class rooms—swept and dusted them and built the fires. He rose at four o'clock in order to get his work done and have time to study his lessons.

He would have been a lawyer, save that the noble purpose of General Armstrong was absorbed by his sensitive nature, and this turned him to be the teacher and the leader of his people.

Perhaps the supreme occasion of Booker T. Washington's life up to this time—supreme because it was the crisis from which he emerged to world-wide reputation and honor—was his great oratorical triumph at the Atlanta Exposition. An eye witness wrote of it:

"There was a remarkable figure—tall, bony, straight as a Sioux chief, high forehead, straight nose, heavy jaws, and strong,

determined mouth, with big, white teeth,
piercing eyes, and a commanding manner.
The sinews stood out on his bronzed neck,
and his muscular right arm swung high in
the air with a lead pencil grasped in the
clinched brown fist.   His voice rang out clear
and true, and he paused impressively as he
made each point.   Within ten minutes the
multitude was in an uproar of enthusiasm.
Handkerchiefs were waved, canes were
flourished, hats were tossed in the air.
The fairest women of Georgia stood up
and cheered.   It was as if the orator had
bewitched them."

It was the chivalry of the white South
cheering the speech of a black man.   It was
a scene worthy of the greatest artist!

God bless Booker T. Washington and his
great institution at Tuskegee!   And may the
poet's prophecy, which he quoted at the close
of his great speech at the unveiling of the
Shaw Monument in Boston, be abundantly
realized in his beloved Southland:

> "They are rising, all are rising—
> The black and the white together."

XXVI.

The Birth of Liberty's Hymn.

I SHALL never forget an afternoon in the Boston Theater on the occasion of an author's readings given in aid of a fund for the Longfellow Memorial. Of the splendid group that were gathered on the platform to read from their own writings three of the stars of the greatest magnitude have been transferred to the sky above the sky.

James Russell Lowell was a most striking figure that afternoon, and read, in addition to a short poem of his own composed for the occasion, Longfellow's "Building of the Ship." He was not a good reader from the elocutionist's point of view, but that splendid head is photographed on my mind, and the tones of his voice come back as though I heard them yesterday.

Oliver Wendell Holmes, cheerful as always, shed gladness from face and eye as a bouquet of lilies exhales fragrance. His reading of " Dorothy Q." gave universal delight.

George William Curtis, the last of that trio of translated literary saints, read from

Mrs. Julia Ward Howe.

" Prue and I " with a graceful dignity which clothed him like an atmosphere.

Among those who still remain none was received with more expressions of pleasure,

and perhaps no reading aroused more enthusiasm, than Julia Ward Howe and her
rendering of "The Battle Hymn of the Republic."

On another occasion I enjoyed her own
story of how that immortal production was
conceived: It was in those stormy times of
1861, when, in company with Dr. S. G.
Howe, her heroic husband, than whom a
more daring and benevolent man America
never produced, Mrs. Howe was visiting
Washington. The city was surrounded on
every side by soldiers, and they had been
compelled to make their way to the capital
through lines of guarding sentries. One
day, in company with Dr. James Freeman
Clarke and his wife, Dr. and Mrs. Howe
were escorted out to the front to see the
army, but were driven back by a sudden attack on the part of the enemy. Mrs. Howe
was greatly impressed by the long lines of
soldiers and the devotion and enthusiasm
which they evinced. They were singing as
they marched "John Brown's Body." James
Freeman Clarke, seeing Mrs. Howe's deep

emotion, which was mirrored in her intense face, said:

" You ought to write some new words to go with that tune."

" I will," she earnestly replied.

She went back to Washington, went to bed, and finally fell asleep. She awoke in the night to find her now famous hymn forming in her brain. It took such tremendous hold upon her that she could not wait until morning, but got up and wrote it down in the gray dawn. What sublime and splendid words she wrote! There is in them the spirit of the old prophets. Nothing could be grander than the first line:

" Mine eyes have seen the glory of the coming of the Lord."

In the second verse one sees through her eyes the vivid picture she had witnessed in her afternoon's visit to the army:

" I have seen Him in the watchfires of a hundred circling camps ;
They have builded Him an altar in the evening dews and damps ;
I can read His righteous sentence by the dim and flaring lamps :
His day is marching on."

In the last two verses there was a triumphant note of daring faith and prophecy that was wonderfully contagious, and millions of men and women took heart again as they read or sang it and caught its optimistic note :

" He has sounded forth the trumpet that shall never call
retreat,
He is sifting out the hearts of men before His judgment
seat :
O be swift, my soul, to answer Him ! be jubilant, my
feet—
     Our God is marching on ! "

This hymn, which was destined to have such world-wide appreciation, won its first victory in Libby Prison. It was printed in the newspapers, and a copy of a paper containing it was smuggled into the prison, where many hundreds of Northern officers and soldiers were confined, among them being the brilliant Chaplain, now Bishop, McCabe. The chaplain could sing anything and make music out of it, but he seized on this splendid battle hymn with a frenzy of delight. It makes the blood in one's veins boil again with patriotic enthusiasm to hear him tell how

the tears rained down strong men's cheeks
as they sang in the Southern prison, far
away from home and friends, those wonderful closing lines:

" In the beauty of the lilies Christ was born across the
sea,
With a glory in His bosom that transfigures you and me :
As He died to make men holy, let us die to make men
free,
While God is marching on."

XXVII.

The Heroism of the Pastor.

THE life of a true Christian minister is like an iceberg at sea, in that by far the largest portion of it is hid from the public gaze. When one thinks of the heroism of a minister he is likely to think only of his faithfulness to conscience and the Gospel in his public sermons or addresses. There is room enough for heroism there, and there have been many conspicuous examples of such courage in the past, and, despite occasional criticisms, I do not believe there is any reason to fear that there is a letting-down in courageous fidelity on the part of the Christian ministry.

The greatest temptation that comes to the minister to be easy and indulgent and lacking in perfect faithfulness is in the opportunities of pastoral work. More souls are won or lost in hand-to-hand or face-to-face struggles than in the public congregations. The temptation to be a pleasant friend, a genial companion, a good fellow, and nothing more, to the members of his congregation is a most insidious one to many ministers of the Gospel. One may be all these and yet

Theodore L. Cuyler, D.D.

have in addition the crowning grace of heroic loyalty to the great mission of his life— to save the souls of his people; to win them to and keep them in personal fellowship with Jesus Christ.

One of the most honored and conspicuous examples of such heroism is witnessed in the career of that Nestor of the American pastorate, Dr. Theodore L. Cuyler. This is the more marked in Dr. Cuyler's case because he has all those qualities which would be likely to tempt one away from what many men regard as the drudgery of pastoral work. His brilliant service in the Christian press is known and read of all men. He is at once the most voluminous and brilliant of all the contributors of religious articles to the newspaper press of the past generation. He has always been in great demand as a preacher and platform speaker. And that, in the face of all this, he has held himself steadily, day by day, through his long pastoral career, to faithful pastoral visitation, in which he has sought with infinite tact and sympathy, and yet with fearless honesty, to warn and rebuke and win men to Christ, is an illustration of the highest heroism.

The result is that there is many a home in Brooklyn to-day where the family altar established, and where Christ reigns supreme, that never could have been captured even by Dr. Cuyler's vivid and forceful sermons, but was stormed and won by that persistent personality that rang the door bell again and again, and reinforced the truth proclaimed on the Sabbath by pungent, heart-searching conversation. Many and many a young man in the "City of Churches" has said to me, while his face glowed with a tender light, "I am one of Dr. Cuyler's boys;" and when these "boys" have come to be grayheaded grandsires, long after the good doctor is wearing his crown in heaven, they will still recall with loving reminiscence the pastor who knew all their names in the big church and made all the children feel that they were his boys and his girls.

In a conversation about pastoral work the good doctor once said to me that, while a sermon scattered like a shotgun, private conversation could be sent straight to its mark, like the ball from a rifle. He relates how he once spent an evening in a vain endeavor

11

to bring a man to a decision for Christ. As
he was about to take his departure the gentleman whom he had been seeking to win
took him up stairs to the nursery to show
the faithful pastor his beautiful children in
their cribs. This was the doctor's golden
opportunity. After looking on the little
sleepers for a moment with loving admiration he turned to his host and said, tenderly,
" Do you mean that these sweet children
shall never have any help from their father
to get to heaven? " The arrow went straight
to its mark. The man was deeply moved,
and in a few weeks became an active member of the church.

Another instance shows Dr. Cuyler's mingled tact and courage in seizing upon an
opportunity to carry his point for the good
of a man's soul. He had called on a rich
merchant in New York on a very cold winter evening. As the door opened for him
to leave the piercing wind swept into the
hallway, and he said, " What an awful night
for the poor! " The merchant shivered at
the remark, and, asking him to wait a

moment, stepped to his library and brought back a roll of bank bills, saying, " Please hand these for me to the poorest people you know." A few days later Dr. Cuyler wrote to the merchant, expressing the grateful thanks of some poor families whom his bounty had relieved in their great distress, and added, " How is it that a man who is so kind to his fellow-creatures has always been so unkind to his Saviour as to refuse him his heart? " That single sentence was blessed of God to the merchant's salvation. He immediately sent for Dr. Cuyler to come and talk with him, and at once gave his heart to the Master. He has been a most valuable and gracious Christian man ever since. He assured Dr. Cuyler that he was the first person that had talked to him about his soul in nearly twenty years. The heroism of the pastor did more than a thousand sermons had been able to do to win him to open loyalty to Christ.

The best part of it all is that this kind of heroism is within the reach of every living ambassador of the Lord.

XXVIII.

"Mother Stewart's" First Glass.

ALTHOUGH Mrs. Thompson, of Hillsboro, O., is known as the mother of the Woman's Christian Temperance Union,

"Mother Stewart."

the famous "Mother Stewart," of Spring-field, in the same State, who was known in the days of her prime as "The Wendell Phillips

in Petticoats," was the immediate cause of
the term, "Temperance Crusade," which
clung to the early stages of the movement of
the women for "God and home and native
land."

One saloon in Springfield was just opposite one of the leading churches, and from the
house where "Mother Stewart" was living
she could see the throng of men going there
in defiance of law. The preacher could
stand in his pulpit and see the people passing
into the saloon during his sermon, and yet
none of the men took hold of the matter to
get evidence against the saloon keeper and
make him obey the law. The incident that
stirred "Mother Stewart" up to act for herself was the sight of a man carrying a sweet-
looking babe in his arms as he went into the
saloon on Sunday morning to get his dram.

" If I had a disguise, I would go in there,"
she said, and asked her landlady if she could
furnish her one. The woman thought a
moment, and then replied, "Yes, I can;"
and brought a large waterproof circular that
enveloped her to her feet. She took off her

glasses, put back her hair, and donned the outfit. She looked like a very respectable old Irish woman. As she passed out she turned to the lady and her daughter and said, "O, now pray for me as you never prayed before in your lives!"

"Mother Stewart" says she was not thinking of danger, but felt buoyed as if she was treading on the air. She passed the third door before reaching the saloon where the drinking was going on. There were young men standing at the counter drinking, and some older men sitting about the place. She desired to make two cases at the same time against the saloon keeper—one for selling distilled liquors by the glass to be drunk on the premises, under the State law, and the other for selling on Sunday, under the city ordinance. But she was afraid to ask for whisky or brandy, lest she might be suspected as a spy. She asked the bartender if she could have something to drink. He asked what she wanted. At a venture she asked if he had any sherry wine. He set a bottle and two small glasses on the counter, one having a little water in it. She did not understand what the water meant; still, she picked up the bottle and started to pour out the wine, but as her hand trembled, and as she wanted to implicate the saloon keeper as much as possible, she requested him to pour it out for her, remarking that she felt rather badly. So he poured it out for her and she asked the price, and he said a dime, which she laid down, and, picking up the glass, walked out.

On the Tuesday evening following that Sunday morning " Mother Stewart " spoke in the church opposite the saloon to an audience that packed it to the doors. Taking her glass of wine, she exhibited it to the people and told the story, " How I bought my first glass of liquor."

That was the beginning of the Temperance Crusade in the city of Springfield, which reached large proportions and did a great amount of good. It was the editor of the *Journal*, of Dayton, O., who named the new movement. He wrote: "One woman in Springfield is disturbing the whole city—

not an unusual thing for a woman to do, however, as they have in times past changed the course of whole empires. The lady to whom we refer is Mrs. Stewart, who is on a Temperance Crusade against liquor selling. She is determined to banish the trade from Springfield, and has got herself reinforced by a battalion of resolute women who are making it hot for the saloon keepers."

And so it was out of the heroism of one motherly woman that the famous phrase, "The Temperance Crusade," was born.

XXIX.

The Call of God.

SOMEHOW, somewhere, some time, God speaks to everyone of us, calling us out of our indifference, to give him our hearts. We may refuse, for we are not mere machines, but we do so at our peril. He does not call us all in the same way. The call came to Samuel as a little child, in the old Jewish tabernacle, in the midnight. It came to Moses, on the back of Mount Horeb, as he herded his father-in-law's sheep. It came to Elisha as he was plowing in the field. It came to Paul on the highway at noon.

I have recently listened to a story of such a call that came to a boy on the bottom of the Ohio River, with the soiled current flowing above him, when he was in imminent danger of his life. A group of lads were in swimming where the Ohio cuts along the line of West Virginia. They were diving from the deck of a small boat or float near

the shore, endeavoring to dive as far down
stream as possible without coming up for
breath.   Just beyond them, farther out in

Rev. George C. Wilding, D.D.

the river, were a half dozen large coal
barges or scows.   One of the lads, the hero
of our present story, dived from the deck
of the float, and, full of ambition to excel

all the other divers of the company, aimed to
go directly down the river with the current;
but in some way he turned slightly toward
the right hand. When his breath was
about exhausted, and he began to feel that
he must come to the surface for air, he began
to rise, and came upward rapidly. To his
surprise and horror his head struck against
something hard.

He soon realized that he was beneath one
of the large coal barges. The blow had
confused him, and he could not determine
which way he had come. It flashed rapidly
through his mind that there was an area of
coal barges in three directions and open
water in the other; but which was the direction of escape he could not make out. Like
lightning came the thought that there were
three chances for death and but one for life,
and that he was uncertain as to the way of
life.

During these quick minutes, or rather
seconds, of electric-like thought there un-
rolled before the eyes of his soul a vivid
panorama of his entire moral life up to that

moment. There did not seem to be haste.
He saw it in itemized detail; nothing seemed
to be omitted, and the most trivial events
stood out with marvelous clearness; each
act and thought of selfish gratification, of
disobedience, of wantonness—none were
missing. And all these accusing deeds were
revealed in their proper moral environment
and background. No one will ever be more
clearly self-condemned on the day of judgment, when an assembled world is gathered
before the great white throne, than was
that West Virginia lad struggling face to
face with death at the bottom of the Ohio
River that summer afternoon.

It is amazing to him, grown now to a man
of middle age, to remember how easily and
clearly he could study and analyze all this,
as, with every faculty alert, he was intently
planning for safety and deliverance. He
felt if he could only know which way the
current was flowing, he would soon find his
way out. Suddenly he remembered having
read somewhere that the current of a stream
flows stronger at the bottom than at the top.

He instantly acted on his thought, and quickly dived to the bottom of the river. He at once thrust his fingers into the soft sediment, and he could, by slowly turning his hands around, feel the movement of the current between his fingers. The sensation of that current sent the blood tingling through his veins, for with it came the chance for life. He now knew the way to the shore. Gathering himself for the effort, he struck, out with all his remaining strength. When he came to the surface he was in the open air. There were the green trees, the blue sky, the fresh air, and the splash and cries of the noisy boys. How beautiful it all looked, and how melodious that babel of sounds!

He swam feebly to the shore and crawled upon a sunny sandbank in a collapsed condition. He swam no more that day, but soon walked home a thoughtful, wiser, and much older boy. He recognized the call of God, and he has followed it from that day. That lad to-day is Dr. George C. Wilding, the eloquent and popular pastor of Hedding

Church, in Jersey City. He has been a wide traveler, and once climbed to the snow-capped peak of Mount Hood and looked far and wide over the glorious panorama of forest and river and mountains of the Northern Sierras; but Dr. Wilding still claims that the highest vision-point and the widest outlook of his life was obtained, not from the pinnacle of Mount Hood, but beneath a coal barge in the muddy bottom of the Ohio River.

XXX.
"Mother Bickerdyke."

THE HEROINE OF THE GRAND ARMY OF THE
REPUBLIC.

MARY A. BICKERDYKE, universally
known as "Mother Bickerdyke," the
unchallenged heroine of the Grand
Army of the Republic, for whom every soldier has a tender place in his heart, is still
living, doing what she can for "the boys,"
in Bunkerhill, Kan. A letter from her,
breathing the spirit of a generation ago, lies
before me while I write.

"Mother Bickerdyke" was called of God to
her work as truly as ever minister was called
to the pulpit, or leaders were reared up by
Divine Providence for a great people. Her
marvelous work for the wounded soldiers
was a labor of love, and her heroism was
born of self-sacrificing devotion that knew
no limit.

After the battle of Shiloh "Mother Bickerdyke" was found one day by one of the

surgeons wrapped in the gray overcoat of a
Confederate officer, for she had disposed of
her shawl to some poor fellow who needed
it. She was wearing a soft slouch hat,

Mary A. Bickerdyke.

having lost her usual shaker bonnet. Her
kettles had been set up, the fire kindled
underneath, and she was dispensing hot soup,
tea, crackers, and other refreshments to the
shivering, fainting, wounded men.

"Where did you get these articles?" the

surgeon inquired, "and under whose authority are you at work?"

She paid no heed to his questions, and probably did not hear them, so completely absorbed was she in her work of mercy. Watching her with admiration for her skill, administrative ability, and intelligence—for she not only fed the wounded men, but dressed their wounds in many cases—the doctor approached her again:

"Madam, you seem to combine in yourself a sick-diet kitchen and a medical staff. May I inquire under whose authority you are working?"

Without pausing in her work she blurted out, "I have received my authority from the Lord God Almighty; have you anything that ranks higher than that?" As a matter of fact, she held no position whatever at that time. She was only a volunteer nurse, and had not yet received an appointment; but her answer revealed the real spirit and purpose of the noble woman.

"Mother Bickerdyke" was always great in an emergency. While stationed at Memphis

12

she found that the people in the enemy's country were charging enormous prices for milk and eggs, and that the most useless produce was being received for hospital supplies. One day she exclaimed to the doctor: "Do you know we are paying fifty cents for every quart of milk we use? and do you know it is such poor stuff—two thirds chalk and water—that if you should pour it into the trough of a respectable pig at home, he would turn up his nose and run off, squealing in disgust?"

"Well, what can we do about it?" asked the doctor.

"If you'll give me thirty days' furlough and transportation, I'll go home and get all the milk and eggs that the Memphis hospitals can use."

"Get milk and eggs! Why, you could not bring them down here if the North would give you all it has. A barrel of eggs would spoil this warm weather before it could reach us; and how on earth could you bring milk?"

"But I'll bring down the milk and egg

producers. I'll get cows and hens, and we'll have milk and eggs of our own. The folks at home, doctor, will give us all the hens and cows we need for the use of these hospitals, and jump at the chance to do it. You needn't laugh or shake your head!" as he turned away, amused and incredulous. "I tell you the people at the North ache to do something for the boys down here, and I can get fifty cows in Illinois alone, for just the asking."

"Pshaw! pshaw!" said the doctor, "you would be laughed at from one end of the country to the other if you should go on so wild an errand."

"Fiddlesticks! who cares for that? Give me a furlough and transportation, and let me try it."

When "Mother Bickerdyke" was in that mood there was only one way out, and North she went. She was escorted as far as St. Louis by several hundred cripples, every one of whom had lost either a leg or an arm. These she saw placed in hospitals, and then went to Chicago. Jacob Strawn, a big-hearted farmer, with a few of his neighbors, gave her a hundred cows at once. In a week after her call rang out the rooms of the Sanitary Commission in Chicago were transformed into a huge hennery.

Before her thirty days' leave of absence was ended "Mother Bickerdyke" returned to Memphis in triumph, amidst the lowing of a hundred cows and the cackling of a thousand hens. Contrabands were detailed to take charge of them; and after that there was an abundance of fresh milk and eggs for the use of the hospitals.

"Mother Bickerdyke" has by no means lost her interest in the old soldier since the war. Mary A. Livermore relates how she expostulated with the dear old woman for getting wet on a stormy day in trying to befriend an old soldier who had been arraigned in the police court on charge of drunkenness. The old heroine bridled in a minute, and retorted, "Mary Livermore, I want you to understand that so long as an old soldier is top of ground he can be sure of two friends—God and me."

XXXI.

The Heroism of the Plodder.

TO my mind there is on the face of the globe no grander specimen of the hero than a boy in that awkward epoch when

Samuel Wilson Naylor.

he can find no place for his hands and his trousers are never long enough to cover his legs, in the midst of pinching poverty, with seemingly no chance for education or culture, who, in such discouraging conditions, fights with clinched teeth his toilsome way through the academy and college and professional school, and stands, ten years later, a splendidly-educated, broadly-cultivated, noble Christian man of the world.

I am going to tell the story of one such hero, because he is a type of thousands of boys and girls in every State of the Union who have heroic stuff in them.

Samuel Wilson Naylor began his fight for an education in 1883, in Washburn College, at Topeka, Kan., in the preparatory department. His family lived on a farm, and for the first half year he boarded at home and went to and fro, five miles every day, and looked after the farm chores night and morning. The rest of the year he did clerical work for a man who gave him in payment a humble room and two meals a day. The third meal, during that time, was always in demand, but was ever a doubtful quantity, and sometimes did not appear. As he had not been able to take Latin during his first year's course, he made up the entire year's work in that language while following a plow during the summer vacation. During 1884 he kept " bachelor's hall " with a young neighbor, the two boys doing their own cooking. In 1885 he was elected mail carrier by the students, and earned enough in this service to pay his board.

In 1886–87 he was elected steward of the boarding club, which again paid for his board. He was also, this year, the business manager of the college paper, and handled it with such care and efficiency that, in addition to paying all his own way, he was able to refund some money which he had borrowed of relatives during the previous years. During 1888 he continued his connection with the college paper and was secretary of the Senate Committee of the State Legislature, for whom he worked only out-of-school hours. In his senior year, 1889, in addition to the business management of the paper, he was United States Census enumerator.

Note that during these years, while he was supporting himself by this hard work, he was by no means lagging in his studies. He won the highest honors in the society debate at the oratorical contest.

In 1890 he went to the Boston University School of Theology. During the first year he was assistant book agent, steward of the boarding club, and occasionally supplied the pulpit of some village church. In 1891 he supported himself in the same way as the previous year, and during the latter part of the year, with three others, organized the Boston University Settlement, which is yet a flourishing institution in the old historic North End of Boston. In 1892 he was field secretary of the University Settlement, which secured his support at the University, and he closed that year by carrying off the honors as the chosen orator of his class.

Let no one imagine that there was no chance for social recognition or literary work under these trying circumstances. In these years he was several times president of a literary society; was president of the college

Young Men's Christian Association during his entire collegiate course of four years; delegate to Moody's Summer School, Northfield, Mass.; and during his senior year was corresponding secretary for the Student Volunteer Movement for Kansas.

At the end of this ten years' constant cultivation of his mind and heart he was in debt only two hundred dollars. This was soon wiped out, and after two years in the pastorate, desiring still further to fit himself for usefulness, he spent a year in foreign travel, visiting Egypt, the Upper Nile, and making a long tour in the Holy Land. He made almost the entire round in Europe on his bicycle, traveling in that economical way over two thousand miles.

Now, this was not genius at all—simply a straightforward, honest lad, with pluck and determination and genuine Christian spirit, who knew how to plod and dig, and who would not be proud of his log-book as I have given it to you. Every church he may serve in the days to come will feel the buoyant strength that he has gained by these years of "blessed drudgery." God bless all the homespun heroes who are making their brave fight for a cultured and larger personality!

XXXII.

A Mission to the Rich.

IT may well be doubted if there is any more thoroughly Christlike work for humanity being accomplished in our time than that which clusters about the social settlements in some of our large cities. The very conception is in the spirit of Him who was rich and yet for our sakes became poor; who put aside the glory of heaven and came down to earth, bringing all His resources of nobility of character, of patience and gentleness of soul, to shed them as a flower does fragrance for the poorest and weakest and meanest of humankind. So the social settlement, placed purposely in the very heart of the slums, where human life is hardest to bear and a glimpse of anything pure and holy is rare indeed, is peopled usually by men and women of culture and refinement, many of whom leave homes of luxury and wealth and for Christ's dear sake deny themselves the happiness of associations to which they have been born and reared in order that by personal example and contact they may make the Christ-life

Miss Jane Addams.

seem possible and beautiful to the most hopeless of their brothers and sisters.

One of the most remarkable of these efforts to bring Christianity incarnate into the heart of poverty and sin is Hull House,

Chicago, and the angel of Hull House is
Miss Jane Addams. It is now ten years
since this institution was founded, and it
has become one of the great institutions of
the city.

Miss Addams's first idea in starting the
work was not so much to help the poor as to
help the rich. Her large soul ached for the
pitiful idleness of many wealthy society girls
who seemed to have no worthy object in life,
and who sadly needed to be brought into
practical sympathy with their fellow-creatures. It has always been her belief that
the work of Hull House benefits the teachers
and workers quite as much as it does the
poor people for whom the service is
rendered. Some of the most enthusiastic
and effective workers in this Christlike service are young women who up to the time
of their becoming interested in this work
had led merely frivolous lives. It has developed and ennobled and glorified them as
much as it has blessed any of the wretched
girls to whom they have ministered with such
tenderness and devotion.

These young women have found that every gift and talent they possess can be brought somewhere into play in this new work. One girl who has been all her life accustomed to the highest world of fashion, and who is an expert in social matters, has displayed a remarkable ability in imparting graceful and elegant manners to young street hoodlums. Another young college girl utterly annihilated the taste for dime novels among the slum boys by a course of talks on the Legends of Charlemagne and his Paladins, which she made so interesting that these urchins, who had never heard an historical lecture in their lives, listened breathless and fascinated. Roland was the hero whose adventures particularly delighted them. After the narration of his death the boys hung about the room disconsolate. At last one remarked, sorrowfully, "Well, it is no use coming any more, Roland's dead!"

But Hull House is not dead; its devoted workers are alive to their finger-tips, and there are brought fresh out of the treasuries of the minds and hearts of these self-sacrifi-

cing women things new and old that capture
the imagination and hold the affection and
enthusiasm of the vigorous young life that
would be otherwise running wild into evil.
The whole object is to present the possibilities of a Christian life, pure and noble,
beautiful and gracious, before eyes to whom
such a life is unknown.

Like all other good things, Hull House
has been a growth.   Ten years ago it consisted of only two young women, who rented
a few rooms in a building that they shared
with a desk manufactory.   But a wonderful
transformation has been wrought.   First,
the desk factory vanished, and Miss Addams
and Miss Starr, with their fellow-residents,
occupied the whole of the old-fashioned Hull
homestead.   Then a wing was added, containing club rooms and lecture halls and
gymnasiums; then another wing at the rear
for a restaurant and public bakery, where
soups, cooked meats, and other edibles could
be had all ready to take home for less than
the price of buying and preparing the raw
material.   Then a children's house was built

to accommodate the day nursery, the kinder-
garten, and the picture gallery. This great
mass of buildings, with all its beehive of
earnest workers and gracious influences, has
been the outcome of the intelligent love and
good will of two Christian women.

Are there not other men and women of
wealth, of college breeding, of rich gifts of
conversation, or of teaching, or of helpful
fellowship, who are weary of simply eating
and drinking and keeping themselves sleek
and comfortable like a fat ox, who will take
courage and heart at this glimpse of a wonderfully rich investment in humanity? For,
after all, the richest investment one can
make in this world, the one that is sure to
pay back the largest dividends on the capital
put in, is an investment in humanity. No
other soil is so fertile, or will yield such
speedy and satisfactory return.

XXXIII.

The Heroism of Faith.

DR. J. WILBUR CHAPMAN, the well-known evangelist, belongs to the roll of honor on which is inscribed the modern " Heroes of the Faith." Dr. Chapman's dominant characteristic is the heroic quality of his faith. He firmly believes that God is able and willing, at any moment, to save any man, rich or poor, learned or ignorant, and instantly transform him from a penitent sinner to a righteous saint. A great many people profess to believe that; but when a man really does believe it, and goes about the world living up to his faith, he is a hero.

Dr. Chapman has great success in reaching men. He is such a simple, straightforward, manly man himself that men believe in him at first glance. At a young men's meeting in Saginaw, Mich., two or three years since, Dr. Chapman was urging men to an immediate decision for Christ. Colonel

13

Bliss, an ex-member of Congress, and one of the wealthiest and most influential citizens of the State, had but just entered the room when the impassioned appeal of the

Dr. J. Wilbur Chapman.

evangelist, " Do it now! Do it now! " fell on his ears. With a sudden impulse, making a decision on the instant, Colonel Bliss arose and simply said, " I will." The whole question of his salvation was settled. The battle he had been waging for years was won. Before a great assemblage of men in Detroit, a few weeks later, he gave this testimony: "I was deeply convicted in my early life—but the war came on. I enlisted and stifled my convictions for the time being. Then I was taken prisoner, and determined that if I was only released, I would be a Christian. My release came, and I said, 'I will wait till the war is ended'—and that came to pass and I was still undecided. Then I said, 'I must give my attention to business, and after I have made a competency I will be a Christian.' I achieved that, but I still delayed. Every day it seemed to grow more difficult, and I had almost lost hope. My conversion seemed an impossibility. But one night I heard Dr. Chapman say the three words, 'Do it now!' And I said, 'That is a message for me,' and with a tremendous effort I stood up and said, 'I will!' Immediately I received a blessing. God certainly revealed himself to me, and from that day I have been more than happy.

And, gentlemen," he said to the five thousand men present, " if you would have the easiest time—the safest time—in fact, God's time to be saved, I repeat the words, ' Do it now! ' "

Colonel Bliss has been a most devoted, enthusiastic Christian ever since.

A very different man was John Pearl, who for thirteen years had scarcely drawn a sober breath, and for the same length of time had not been in the church, except occasionally to attend a funeral. His family had been broken up through his sin, and he had led as dissolute a life as one could possibly follow. All his earnings were spent in the saloons; he was profane, and sinful, in fact, in almost every way common to man. People who knew him thought him hardly worth saving, and so he had been practically forsaken by Christians.

Dr. Chapman was holding revival meetings in Greenbush, just across the river from Albany, N. Y. One evening John Pearl was sitting in a saloon when some one said, " Chapman is preaching in the Presbyterian church to-night." This arrested Pearl's attention, and he said, "I'll go and hear him." The bystanders laughed at the idea of old John Pearl going to church, but he started out. When he reached the church his courage failed him. He said to himself, "No one will want me. I am nothing but a poor drunkard. I am dirty and almost in rags." And so he hurried away to the saloon. But God would not let him go, and he was soon back again at the church door. Almost before he knew it he was in the church and in the second pew from the front. For a part of the service he seemed stupefied; then he began to give the truth his attention, and when the invitation was given his was the first hand lifted. In the after meeting he was the first to fall upon his knees; there God met him, and he was wonderfully converted.

John Pearl became a member of the church, and has been a faithful, loyal follower of Jesus Christ ever since. Only once has he been tempted to drink. One day the devil made a dead set for his soul. It

seemed as if the tiger thirst for strong drink
would drive him wild, but, like Joseph in
Potiphar's palace, he fled from the face of
his temptation, and, going home, he cried
unto God for deliverance. His cry was
heard, and from that day until this he has
been entirely free from the appetite for
strong drink. His life seems to flow on as
sweetly and securely as if he had never
known thirteen years of misery and wretchedness.

I have chosen these two cases, standing
in such strong contrast, out of the thousands
of men who have been led to Christ through
the charming brotherliness and heroic faith
of Dr. Chapman's ministry.

XXXIV.

Clara Barton on the Battlefield.

THE heroism of Miss Clara Barton in going to Armenia to carry relief to the persecuted Christians of that devoted land in an hour so dark with danger that strong men feared to trust themselves in the power of the inhuman Turk, was so conspicuous as to make in itself a reputation worthy of a lifetime of service.

It is well, however, for the younger portion of our readers to have their attention called to the fact that Miss Barton's fearless service in Armenia was but the mature flowering of a heroic life. The War of the Rebellion brought to the front no character more conspicuously brave and self-denying than hers.

Dr. Brockett, in his *Heroines of the Rebellion*, relates a circumstance which occurred during the battle of Fredericksburg that strikingly illustrates the courage of Miss Barton in the presence of danger. In the skirmishing of the 12th of December, the day preceding the great and disastrous battle, a part of the Union troops had crossed over to Fredericksburg, and after a brief

Clara Barton.

fight had driven back a body of Confederates, wounding and capturing a number of them, whom they sent as prisoners across the river to Falmouth, where Miss Barton as yet had her camp. The wounded Confederates were brought to her for care and

treatment. Among them was a young officer, mortally hurt. Though she could not
save his life, she ministered to him as
well as she could, partially stanching his
wound, quenching his raging thirst, and
endeavoring to make his condition as comfortable as possible. Just at this time an
orderly arrived with a message from the
medical director of the Ninth Army Corps,
requesting her to come over to Fredericksburg and organize the hospitals and diet
kitchens for the corps. The officer heard
the request, and, beckoning to her, for he
was too weak to speak aloud, he whispered
a request that she would not go. She replied that she must do so; that her duty
to the corps to which she was attached required it. "Lady," he replied, "you have
been very kind to me. You could not save
my life, but you have endeavored to render
death easy. I owe it to you to tell you
what a few hours ago I would have died
sooner than have revealed. The whole ar-
rangement of the Confederate troops and
artillery is intended as a trap for your

people. Every street and lane of the city is covered by our cannon. They are now concealed, and do not reply to the bombardment of your army because they wish to entice you across. When your entire army has reached the other side of the Rappahannock and attempts to move along the streets it will find Fredericksburg only a slaughter pen, and not a regiment of it will be allowed to escape. Do not go over, for you will go to certain death!"

While her tender sensibilities prevented her from adding to the sufferings of the dying man by not apparently heeding his warning, Miss Barton did not on account of it forego for an instant her intention of sharing the fortunes of the Ninth Corps on the other side of the river. The poor fellow was almost gone, and, waiting only to close his eyes to the battlefields of earth, she crossed on the frail bridge and was welcomed with cheers by the Ninth Corps, who looked upon her as their guardian angel. She remained with them until the evening of their retreat, and, with the fidelity of a faithful sea captain, who is always the last to leave his vessel in time of shipwreck, she refused to return until all the wounded men of the corps in the hospitals were safely across the river.

At another time Miss Barton arrived in the rear of the battle and found that the army medical supplies had not come. The small stock of dressings was exhausted, and the surgeons were trying to make bandages of corn husks. Miss Barton opened to them her stock of dressings, and proceeded with her companions to distribute food among the wounded and fainting. When her bread was all gone she took the meal in which her bottles of medicine had been packed and began to make gruel. When this was exhausted she searched the cellar of a farmhouse near by and discovered three barrels of flour and a bag of salt which the Confederates had hidden the day before. Kettles were found about the house, and she prepared to make gruel on a large scale, which was carried in buckets and distributed along the line for miles. Although the battle raged fiercely, and her face became as black as a Negro's and her lips and throat parched with the smoke, she kept her place mixing the gruel until nightfall ended the battle. But darkness only brought new terror to the suffering, for as the night closed in the surgeon in charge at the old farmhouse looked despairingly at a bit of candle, and said it was the only one on the place; and no one could stir till morning. A thousand men lay around dangerously wounded and suffering terribly from thirst, and many must die before the light of another day. It was a fearful thing to die alone and in the dark, and no one could move among the wounded for fear of stumbling over them. Then it was that Miss Barton's forethought and womanly housekeeping shone out. She gladdened the eyes of the astonished surgeon by bringing out thirty lanterns and an abundance of candles which she had thoughtfully provided for just such an emergency. But for those lanterns many a life would have gone out in the darkness that night that by their aid was saved to bless home circles after the war was ended.

It will take Clara Barton a long time after she gets to heaven to greet all the people who have been comforted and blessed by her heroic life.

XXXV.
The Last of the Hutchinsons.

OF all that heroic group in which Phillips and Lovejoy and Garrison and Whittier and many others were shining stars there was no more unique inner circle than what was known as " The Hutchinson Family." They were not orators, but they were sweet singers, who were able to send the gospel of liberty into many a heart that was locked and barred against the most persuasive key of public speech.

Mr. John Wallace Hutchinson, the last left on earth of that truly brave and picturesque group, has recently published a *Story of the Hutchinsons*, brimful of fascinating reminiscences of a brave and romantic time.

Mr. Hutchinson tells this story of Henry Clay: It was in the year 1848, and " The Hutchinsons" were in New York giving concerts. Jesse, one of the brothers, wrote a new song of Mr. Clay, entitled " Harry of the West," and the present survivor wrote the music for it. This song was prepared on their way to New York, and was first sung on the boat between New Haven and that city.

John Wallace Hutchinson.

While in New York they were invited by Captain Knight, of the then new and famous ship, *Henry Clay*, to go on board his vessel. Complying, they went into the captain's cabin, and, standing in a group, they struck up their new song. They had hardly finished when an alderman of the city who was on board said to them, enthusiastically, "You must go and sing that song to Henry Clay this afternoon."

Going ashore, they soon arrived at the hotel, where a great reception was taking place. The mayor, his chief counselors, and their distinguished guest were just about taking their wine at the banquet when the singers were ushered in. The mayor at once arose, announcing their presence, and asked them to sing an appropriate selection. The four brothers sang:

> " Come, brothers, now let's hurry out
>   To see our honored guest,
> For lo, in every street they shout,
>   Brave ' Harry of the West.'
>
> " For th' glorious day is coming near
>   When wrong shall be redressed,
> And freedom's star shine bright and clea;
>   On ' Harry of the West.'
>
> " Then hail, all hail, thrice-honored sage,
>   Our most distinguished guest !
> We'll venerate thy good old age,
>   Brave ' Harry of the West.'"

While they were singing this song Mr. Clay's eyes opened and his chin dropped with surprise. At the close he arose and came to them, saying, "What can I do to repay you for this great honor you have conferred upon me?" Subsequently he sent his wine down to them, but the brave young Hutchinsons sent him back word that they were teetotalers and could not drink with him. It took a good deal more courage to do that in 1848 than it would now. On receiving their reply Henry Clay arose from the table for the second time, and, leaving the circle of politicians about him, walked across the room, the observed of all observers, and said to the young singers, "If I were a young man like yourselves, I'd be a teetotaler too."

John Wallace Hutchinson has remained faithful to his temperance principles through all the years, and his handsome head, as splendid as Nathaniel Hawthorne's, often graces the platform of a temperance meeting.

14

XXXVI.

The Deaconesses' Sheet Fund.

THERE are many kinds of heroism. The most common kind and the sort that is most readily appreciated is the dashing,

Mrs. Anna E. Hull.

aggressive onslaught on the enemy- some picturesque undertaking like Sheridan's

ride from Winchester, a scene which lends
itself easily to the canvas of the painter,
the tongue of the orator, or the pen of the
poet. Then there is another sort that we
can all easily understand—the heroism of
self-sacrifice. There is also the quieter, but
none the less sublime, heroism of the saint
in the bondage of affliction—one with a soul
large and strong and full of divine longing
for the performance of noble deeds and
splendid achievement, that is shut in like
Joseph in the Egyptian dungeon, or Paul in
Nero's prison in Rome, or some fragile
woman chained to her sick bed through
weary months of lingering illness.

There is a heroism of still another kind—
it is the heroic spirit exhibiting itself in little things that may help to sweeten human
existence. I have just discovered a woman
illustrating this remarkably helpful sort of
heroism.

Mrs. Anna E. Hull is the large-souled
and genial-natured secretary of the Young
Woman's Christian Association in the city
of Cleveland, O. She is one of those strong,

warm natures which seem to gather as they go through youth and middle age rich sheaves of experience and wisdom, which it is their joyous ability to impart to the young, who find in them friend and leader. I remember that in one of Phillips Brooks's great sermons he says that every experience of trial and grief we pass through in life and come out, by the strength of God, victorious we are given the key to that trial, and are ever after able to unlock it and show the way through to others. When I see a woman like Mrs. Hull, about whom young girls who are away from home and mother and the guarding associations of home life flock for sympathy and wisdom, I seem to see in her cultivated, sympathetic helpfulness the shining keys hanging at the girdle that are able to unlock many a doorway that seems forbidding and lead trembling feet through in safety to the brighter life beyond.

Mrs. Hull was at a Home Missionary meeting not long ago, and she heard a little talk given by one of the nurse deaconesses concerning a poor sick woman whom she was nursing. The woman was very worthy, but extremely poor, not even having sheets for the bed. The deaconess went on to relate how often it was the case in the homes of the very poor that the luxury of clean sheets was unknown, even in cases of severe illness.

The statement of the deaconess was a revelation to Mrs. Hull. She had known, of course, that the very poor must suffer many privations; but it had not occurred to her that here and there through the city were many sufferers who in times of hot fever and painful restlessness never knew the soothing comfort that comes from drawing cool, spotless sheets over the fevered body. As the good woman listened to the story of the deaconess she remembered that at that very moment there were some fine sheets lying in her trunk, souvenirs from her own happy housekeeping days now gone by, and she felt ashamed that they should be folded away in camphor while God's poor children suffered for need of them.

She immediately went home and took the sheets out and sent them at once to the Deaconess Home. Then she put a box on her writing desk and marked it " The Deaconesses' Sheet Fund," and the money that can be spared goes into it, and her friends add to it as they can, and every time enough is gathered to buy a pair of sheets they are purchased and hemmed and go on their way of loving ministration. God bless the Sheet Fund and multiply the people who shall endeavor with the same heroic cheerfulness to attack the lesser demons that afflict poor humanity!

XXXVII.
Grandpa Sampson's Mail Bag.

FOR more than twenty years Rev. William Sampson has been the chaplain and superintendent of the Children's Aid So-

Rev. William Sampson.

ciety and Industrial School and Home in the city of Cleveland, O. He was an old man when he came, but these twenty years of caring for little children have freshened him and renewed his youth, so that, though the almanac says he is eighty-three, the glow of immortal youth is on his heart and in his eyes.

There is no work more fascinating or more full of promise and hope for the future than that which ministers to the needs of poor and homeless children. Every little child that comes into a home like this has some interesting story. Drunken parents and other evils degrade and bring many families to poverty and wretchedness. Although surrounded with vice and misery, the child is not to blame. In other cases the mother dies and the father is unable to keep the children together. Because of these and many other reasons little waifs are thrown out, and, like the Master who loves them, have no place to lay their heads. In his spirit, in his dear name, William Sampson exults with a mother-like tenderness over every such child with as much eagerness as a gold miner who has found a precious nugget.

In this home they are taught habits of cleanliness, civility of manners, respect for age, and the sanctity of religious worship, together with such industries as are adapted to their capacity. Over five thousand children have received instruction and help in the years that are gone, and over twenty-six hundred of these boys and girls have been placed in good homes in different parts of the country, where they have had a fair chance for noble lives.

These lads and lasses, happily placed in good homes, out on the farms and in the villages of the great West, shower their loving letters on this good man who has been such a benediction to them. I have been peering into this mail bag, and the letters are so fresh and redolent of breezy farm-life and sincere childish affection that one cannot wonder that Grandpa Sampson renews his youth as he reads them. Here is one from a boy, from which I take these lines: "I had a swamp that brought me $7.25. I put it to corn and potatoes, and had fourteen bushels of corn and twenty bushels of potatoes." Then he adds something about the pure life of that country settlement. "I want to tell you about my surroundings. There is not a man in this locality who has any bad habits, such as drink and profane language." Not a bad place that for a young lad of fourteen!

Here is a little girl who bubbles over with: "I am happy as a bird, and I go to school every day, and I have such a good teacher. I sold my lamb and I got three dollars for it; now I have got four dollars and twenty cents."

Here is a pathetic little touch in a letter from a little colored boy: "How many children have you? How many colored boys and girls? I am trying to be good, grandpa, so that when I die I may meet you in heaven."

All through these letters, and at the close of every one of them, there are expressions like these: "Love to you, grandpa;" "I love you, and would like to have your picture;" "I shall always have pleasant memories of you, you dear Grandpa Sampson;"

" Thank God that he raised up Grandpa Sampson ! " " Lots of love to grandpa ! " and so on with ever-varying phrase, but breathing the same spirit of gratitude and love.

This mail bag is Grandpa Sampson's constant garden of delight.   I never see him without thinking how happy this old Christlike hero will be in heaven, where so many children are gathering every year.

XXXVIII.
Before the King.

NO society of modern times has done so much to develop American women and arouse in them the heroic qualities as the Woman's Christian Temperance Union.

Mary Clement Leavitt.

Mary Clement Leavitt was the first messenger to carry the White Ribbon banner

around the world, and proclaim its total-ab-
stinence gospel in far-away lands. She once
told me a most interesting story of her visit
to the King of Siam: Mrs. Leavitt had been
in Siam for some time, but had had no opportunity to see the king, as his majesty
was absent from the city. Just before her
departure, however, the king returned, and
within six hours he sent her a messenger,
saying that he would give her an audience
at six o'clock next day, and ordering Mr.
Bradley, the English interpreter, the son of
an American missionary, to attend and in-
terpret the conversation. Everything in
Siam goes by order, and not by request.

Mrs. Leavitt arrived at the exact moment,
and was shown into an anteroom decorated
with armor from many countries. The new
Italian Minister was with his majesty, so
they had to wait a few minutes. Presently
they passed up into a room of pinkish
tinge, ornamented with gold; a smiling
young gentleman came toward the temperance orator, and taking her by the hand,
led her to the center of the room and

into the immediate presence of the King of Siam.

The king spoke English well and understood it perfectly; but he would not converse in a language that his courtiers could not understand, so he talked in Siamese through an interpreter.

Their conversation immediately began on the purpose of her mission around the world. The king agreed with Mrs. Leavitt that it would be well for his kingdom if never a drop of liquor should enter it again. He was himself a total abstainer, but even his example had not been enough to keep his half-brothers (there were about seventy of them) from following the bad example of the foreign diplomats. When the White Ribboner suggested to him that he might make total abstinence a prerequisite for promotion, his majesty, with a smile and a peculiar look around upon the thirty-five or forty courtiers who were in attendance, said: " I have never thought of that. I will meditate upon it, and I think I will act upon it." In reply to her query, if he could not prohibit the introduction of liquor into his country, he said it would be easy enough with China, whence most of it came, but with regard to England and France it would require deep thought and great diplomacy, or the greatest evils would be brought upon him.

Speaking of Christianity, the king turned to her and said, " But your Christian religion allows the use of intoxicating liquor; how, then, can you work for its entire suppression?" She explained the new line along which she was working and in which she thoroughly believed, to which his majesty responded: " I am very glad to hear this, for I have often wondered why a religion so superior to all others, except as to drink, should fall below ours [the Buddhist] and the Mohammedan in that particular. It is much to be hoped that this new view will prevail, and that all missionaries will teach it, especially in Buddhistic countries."

The king had learned his English from the Bible as his text-book under the instruction of Mr. Bradley, an American missionary. It appeared to Mrs. Leavitt that he believed the Christian religion to be the true one, and that he wished to see it spread in his kingdom, for he said often to the missionaries: "Teach as many women and children as you can. It is a good religion for women and children." He was far too astute a man not to know that the religion which was taught to women and children would permeate everywhere, but the tenure by which he held his throne was the vow he had taken on himself to support the religion of Buddha.

At the time of Mrs. Leavitt's visit the present king was only a lad of twelve years, and was said to be a very gifted boy. It is her opinion that if he inaugurates as many reforms as his father did, the kingdom will approach the status of a Christian country. Up to the time of his father's reign all who came into the presence of the King of Siam were required to come creeping on hands and knees; but immediately after his coronation when the people came before him in this way he took the first one, who happened to be his uncle, by the hand and lifted him up, and forbade anyone ever again to come before him in that manner. He said, " I am your king, and expect your obedience; but I am a man, and must not be worshiped."

Mrs. Leavitt's spirituelle face and earnest eyes, in which shines the fire of an undying energy, bring to mind the promise in the Book of Proverbs concerning the diligent soul, that such an one " shall stand before kings."

15

XXXIX.

A Hero from the Wigwam.

THE appearance of Chief Joseph, who is perhaps the most famous American Indian now alive, at the Grant Memorial exercises in New York city recalled to my mind very interesting personal reminiscences. Chief Joseph and myself are natives of the same splendid mountain region in the Northwest, and, though he is a number of years older, through all my boyhood I had a great admiration for him, and have often seen him in his younger manhood, when he was as fine a specimen of the plains chieftain as could be imagined. Absence from the Western mountains has given me a sort of fellow-feeling with Chief Joseph. When I read some years since of his plea to the army officers, made at a time when he was confined down in the flat, sickly Indian Territory, " Give me just one little mountain and I will die content! " I could not restrain the tears of sympathy.

Joseph fought for that which the white man calls patriotism when it has been crowned with success. His father received all the early explorers and settlers with un-

Chief Joseph.

suspicious generosity and in the spirit of a broad, manly fellowship. The Nez Perces prided themselves on having received Lewis and Clarke, Bonneville, Fremont, and other white men with the hand of friendship, and on never having falsified their promises. Up to the time of Joseph's outbreak, though a number of Nez Perces had been killed by white men, only one white man had ever fallen at the hand of a Nez Perce.

Joseph's father joined with the other independent chiefs in a formal treaty, concluded in the Walla Walla Valley in 1855, by which the Indians gave up all claims to certain large tracts of land. Old Joseph entered into this contract on the express stipulation that the Wallowa and Imnaha Valleys should remain to him and his children forever. Soon the white men wanted these valleys, and another treaty was made with several chiefs, but Joseph refused to have anything to do with it, and was not even present; but these valleys that had been guaranteed to Joseph on the honor of the United States Government were by this new treaty taken from him. Joseph's own parable, by which he illustrated the cruel injustice of this treatment, cannot be improved upon. Said he: " A man comes to me and says, ' Joseph, I like your horses, and I want to buy them.'   I say, ' I do not want to sell them.'   Then he goes to my neighbor and says, ' Joseph has some good horses, but he will not sell them,' and my neighbor says, ' Pay me and you may have them.'   And he does so, and then comes to me and says, ' Joseph, I have bought your horses.' "

Despite all justice and reason, marauders poured into this beautiful country, the home of his youth, and United States troops were sent to compel Joseph and his people to remove to a strange reservation.   Imagine the agony of brave-hearted men and women in an emergency like that!   Yet with a breaking heart Joseph concluded to move.   In his own language he says: "I said in my heart that rather than have war I would give up my country.   I would give up everything rather than have the blood of white men upon the hands of my people."

It was not easy for Joseph to bring his people to consent to move.   The young men wished to fight.   At this time Chief Joseph rode one day through his village with a revolver in each hand, saying he would shoot the first one of his warriors who should resist the government. Finally they gathered together their herds of cattle and horses and began to move. A storm came and raised the river so high that some of the cattle could not be taken across. Indian guards were put in charge of the cattle left behind. White men attacked these guards and drove away the cattle. Joseph could no longer restrain his men; that was the birth of the Nez Perce Indian war.

Nothing in the history of modern warfare surpasses in daring, genius, and bravery the exploits of Joseph, the Nez Perce chief. General O. O. Howard, who conducted the great pursuit, pays the highest possible tribute to his generalship. Joseph, after being defeated in a bitterly-contested battle, led his great caravan of two thousand horses or more, on which were women and children, the aged, the wounded, the palsied, and blind, by a seemingly impossible trail, interlaced with fallen trees, through the most rugged mountains to the Bitter Root

Valley, where, with the cool wisdom of a Von Moltke or a Grant, he made a treaty of forbearance with the inhabitants, passing by settlements containing banks and stores, and near farms rich with stock, but taking nothing and hurting no one.   So he pushed on; he crossed the Rocky Mountains twice, the Yellowstone and Missouri Rivers, and was within one day's march of Canada when he was taken.

During all this time the United States Government had thousands of soldiers in the field, under veteran officers, and had spent many millions of dollars in coping with this brave young hero.

Yes, why not say hero?   If we were reading of Roman or Grecian wars, we should certainly consider it something magnificent in a race that had been trodden under foot for a hundred years that it was still able to compel such respect for its patriotic devotion to home and kindred.

If Joseph had been of less noble spirit, he need never have suffered capture.   He himself says: "We could have escaped if we

had left our wounded behind. We were un-
willing to do this." And then he adds, with
bitter sarcasm, "We had never heard of a
wounded Indian recovering while in the
hands of white men." A little company
did slip away and escaped across the line.
When the government sent a commissioner
over there to ask them to come back a squaw
named "The-one-that-speaks-once," wife of
"The-man-that-scatters-the-bear," stood up
in the council and said: "I was over at
your country. I wanted to raise my children over there, but you did not give me
any time. I came over to this country to
raise my children and to have a little peace."

I hope that Joseph may grow old grace-
fully, and that it may be true of him that
"at evening time there shall be light."

XL.

The Author of Memorial Day.

SURELY no one thing has done so much to soften the bitterness which civil war left in our country as the beautiful

Mrs. John A. Logan.

ceremonies connected with Memorial Day. As the years have gone on, and every Memorial Day the Southern soldiers have been more and more wont to cover the graves of their dead foemen with wreathes of Southern flowers, and again and again gray-haired veterans from both the "Blue and the Gray" have met beside the Hudson to do honor to the great commander who at Appomattox said, "Let us have peace," the cold mists of suspicion and distrust have blown away, until again we see eye to eye.

Mrs. John A. Logan, the wife of the heroic volunteer general, and herself a brave personality, has given me the story of the conception of Memorial Day. In company with Colonel Charles L. Wilson, of Chicago, then editor of the Chicago *Journal*, his niece, Miss Anna Wilson (now Mrs. Horatio May, of Chicago), and a Miss Farrar, Mrs. Logan made a trip in March, 1868, to Richmond for the purpose of visiting the fortifications and battlefields around that city. General Logan was to have accompanied them, but could not leave his duties in the House of Representatives to do so, as some important measure was pending at that juncture.

When they returned they reported to him
all that they had seen during their visit.
Among other things Mrs. Logan was particularly impressed by the evidences of des-
olation and destruction which she witnessed
everywhere, but which seemed to her to be
particularly emphasized by the innumerable
graves which filled the cemeteries, many
of which were those of Confederate soldiers.
In the summer before they had all been
decorated by wreaths of flowers and little
flags, all of which were faded, but which
seemed to the tender-hearted woman to be a
mute evidence of the devotion and gratitude
of those people to the men who had lost
their lives for their cause.

In speaking of this General Logan said
that it was not an original custom with the
people of the South ; that the classics are full
of descriptions of the customs of the ancients
in decorating the graves and cinerary urns
of their dead ; and that he considered it a
most beautiful custom and one worthy to be
copied, and, as he was then commander-in-
chief of the Grand Army of the Republic,

that he intended issuing an order, asking the entire people of the nation to inaugurate the custom of annually decorating the graves of the patriotic dead as a memorial to their sacrifice and devotion to country.

He issued the first order for May 30th, 1868, and it was so enthusiastically received and generally observed that he decided to cause it to be a national holiday by a joint resolution of Congress, and to make it one of the duties of the commanders of the Grand Army of the Republic to issue an order every year for its observance. And through his efforts this was accomplished, and has passed into history and made a beautiful custom perpetual.

Mrs. May is now the only living member, besides Mrs. Logan, of the party whose visit to Richmond was the immediate cause of a general call for a Memorial Day. General Chipman was then adjutant-general of the Grand Army of the Republic, and General Logan sent for him, and they talked the matter over, and the order was signed by General Logan and General Chipman as his adjutant-general of the Grand Army of the Republic. It was then the intention, also, to secure an appropriation every year from Congress to publish the proceedings of Memorial Day, so as to compile in that way the patriotic addresses that might be made; but they became so voluminous that it was found impracticable; and hence there was but one volume issued, this being entitled *National Memorial Day*. It was edited by Major Fachtes, who is also now dead.

It will thus be seen that Memorial Day was born out of a partnership between a woman's tender heart and a man's noble purpose. It is also sweet to reflect that South and North united at its birth. The Southern mourners were the first to cover the graves of their dead with flowers, and their Northern brothers to call to it national attention and make the custom as wide as the country.

BOOKS BY DR. LOUIS ALBERT BANKS.

The Christ Brotherhood. 12mo, cloth, gilt top, 323 pp., $1.20.

All who are acquainted with Dr. Banks's work in the ministry, both East and West, will at once recognize his fitness to treat the interesting and important subjects associated with Christian brotherliness. Like all of his books, this one is full of incident and graphic illustrations, and abounds in suggestive material, valuable to every public speaker.

The Christ Dream. 12mo, cloth, gilt top, 275 pp., $1.20.

A series of twenty-four sermons in which illustrations of the Christ ideal are thrown upon the canvas, showing here and there individuals who have risen above the selfish and measure up to the Christ dream. In tone it is optimistic, and sees the bright side of life.

Heavenly Trade-Winds. A Volume of Sermons. 12mo, cloth, 351 pp., $1.25.

"The sermons included in this volume have all been delivered in the regular course of my ministry in the Hanson Place Methodist Episcopal Church, Brooklyn. They have been blessed of God in comforting the weary, giving courage to the faint, arousing the indifferent, and awakening the sinful."—*Author's Preface*.

Heroic Personalities. Illustrated. 12mo, cloth, 200 pp., $1.00.

Treats of striking and heroic incidents in the lives of forty men and women. These are not mere biographical sketches, but each chapter contains a striking story of great possible value as illustrative material.

Common Folks' Religion. A Volume of Sermons. 12mo, cloth, 343 pp., $1.50.

Dr. Banks presents Christ to the "common people," and preaches to everyday folk the glorious everyday truths of the Scripture.

The People's Christ. A Volume of Sermons and Other Addresses and Papers. 12mo, cloth, 220 pp., $1.25.

Their manner of presenting Christian truth is striking.

Christ and His Friends. A Collection of Revival Sermons, Simple and Direct, and Wholly Devoid of Oratorical Artifice, but Rich in Natural Eloquence, and Burning with Spiritual Fervor. 12mo, cloth, gilt top, 390 pp., $1.50.

The author has strengthened and enlivened them with many illustrations and anecdotes.

The Saloon-Keeper's Ledger. The Business and Financial Side of the Drink Question. 12mo, cloth, 129 pp., 75 cents.

Among the items treated are : The Saloon Debtor to Disease, Private and Social Immorality, Ruined Homes, Lawlessness and Crime, and Political Corruption.

White Slaves; or, The Oppression of the Worthy Poor. Fifty illustrations. 12mo, cloth, 327 pp., $1.50.

The Rev. Dr. Banks has made a personal and searching investigation into the homes of the poorer classes, and in *White Slaves* the results are given.

The Fisherman and His Friends. 12mo, cloth, gilt top, 365 pages, $1.50.

A companion volume to *Christ and His Friends*, consisting of thirty-one stirring revival discourses, full of stimulus and suggestion for ministers, Bible class teachers, and all Christian workers and others who desire to become proficient in the supreme capacity of winning souls to Christ. They furnish a rich store of fresh spiritual inspiration, their subjects being strong, stimulating, and novel in treatment, without being sensational or elaborate. They were originally preached by the author in a successful series of revival meetings, which resulted in many conversions.

Hero Tales from Sacred Story. The Romantic Stories of Bible Characters Retold in Graphic Style, with Modern Parallels and Striking Applications. Richly illustrated with 19 full-page half-tone illustrations from Famous Paintings. 12mo, cloth, gilt top, 279 pp., $1.50.

" One cannot imagine a better book to put into the hands of a young man or young woman than this."

Seven Times Around Jericho. 12mo, buckram, 134 pp., 75 cents.

Seven strong and stirring temperance discourses, in which deep enthusiasm is combined with rational reasoning—a refreshing change from the conventional temperance arguments. Pathetic incidents and stories are made to carry most convincingly their vital significance to the subjects discussed. They treat in a broad manner various features of the question.

The Honeycombs of Life. A Volume of Sermons. 12mo, cloth, 397 pp., $1.50.

Most of the discourses are spiritual honeycombs, means of refreshment and illumination by the way. The volume is well laden with evangelical truth and breathes a holy inspiration. This volume includes Dr. Banks's memorial tribute to Lucy Stone and his powerful sermon in regard to the Chinese in America, entitled " Our Brother in Yellow."

Revival Quiver. A Pastor's Record of Four Revival Campaigns. 12mo, cloth, 254 pp., $1.50.

This book is, in some sense, a record of personal experiences in revival work. It begins with " Planning for a Revival," followed by " Methods in Revival Work." This is followed by brief outlines of some hundred or more sermons. They have points to them, and one can readily see that they were adapted to the purpose designed. The volume closes with " A Scheme of City Evangelization." It seems to us a valuable book, adapted to the wants of many a preacher and pastor.

Sermon Stories for Boys and Girls. 12mo, cloth, 218 pp., $1.00.

" The sermon stories which make up this volume have been gathered out of the current of life, and told in my own way to the children of the congregations where I have ministered from time to time."
—*Author's Preface.*

An Oregon Boyhood. 12mo, cloth, 173 pp., $1.25.

Dr. Banks takes his readers into an entirely new field in *An Oregon Boyhood*, in which he gives the present generation a description of the scenes and adventures of boyhood and youth in that far Western country.

240

22 W

www.ingramcontent.com/pod-product-compliance
Lightning Source LLC
Chambersburg PA
CBHW020100030726
47498CB00006B/2002